Family Mistakes

Ellie McLellan Genealogy Mystery - Book 2

Beth Farrar

Edited by Ronnie Pelletier

Cover by GetCovers.com

First edition published – 2023

eBook ISBN: 978-1-7386664-2-3

Paperback ISBN: 978-1-738664-3-0

Hardcover ISBN: 978-1-738664-5-4

No part of this book was written by AI – just a human's blood, sweat and tears (and lots of stress!)

Author's Note: Being a Canadian author, please excuse any double "l"s or wayward "u"s in words, eh. Please do not flag them. Much appreciated.

Also By

Ellie McLellan Genealogy Mystery Series

Family Secets - Book 1

Family Mistakes – Book 2

Family Promises – Book 3

Contents

My family are my ground. Our roots will always be entwined, and I would never have it any other way. You guys are the best family anyone could ever have. Thank you for the excitement!

Chapter One

Ruth Cotter clutched the tattered old envelopes tight to her chest. She stared out the kitchen window, past the rain pattering against the glass and off into the past. Back seventy-five years to the young man who had written of his love for her while fighting in WWII.

"This means he wanted me," she whispered, dragging her gaze away from the storm outside to scan the pages that had just shattered her quietly lived life into pieces.

A storm now raged inside her heart.

"*My darling, Ruth. The thought of holding you once again in my arms is the only thing getting me through these days of horror. A lifetime of being by your side is the only remedy I see.*"

"He must have come here to see me after the war. How is that possible?" She turned at the sound of her sister's squeaky shoes against the hardwood hallway floor, the first human sound she'd heard this entire night of studying the batch of letters she'd received so unexpectedly at last night's seniors genealogy meeting.

"Have you recovered from your faint?" Ruth asked.

"I was dehydrated, but I'm fine now."

Accepting the answer, Ruth plowed ahead with her own concerns. "Listen to this, Shirley." Ruth shook a page at her before pushing her glasses up her nose to focus on a section. "He says he's going to ask Father for my hand, and he sees no future without me in it." Her eyes shone with hope. "Did I miss him? Did he come here and I missed him?"

Shirley stood in the kitchen doorway. She murmured, "I have no idea."

"No idea? You didn't know about these letters?" Ruth's eyes narrowed as she sought to make sense of what was burning in her hands. Her future had rested on the black ink on these pages. A future with a home, family, a life with the man she had loved with her whole heart, and still loved after seventy-five years.

"Never seen them before." Shirley eased from one foot to the other.

A tinge of pink appeared in Shirley's normally pale cheeks, and it seemed to Ruth her sister wouldn't look her in the eye. Was Shirley lying? Abruptly, Ruth's confusion vanished. She studied her sister, the thoughts running through her mind too horrible to believe.

"Then *who* would do such a thing as hide these letters from me?"

Shirley froze like a deer in the headlights. "Maybe it was Dad." She tossed the thought back at Ruth.

"Dad?" Ruth let out an unbelieving snort. "Dad would *never* hurt me like this."

"He didn't like Jeremy, you know that."

"I did *not* know that." Ruth sank onto a kitchen chair, not trusting her legs to hold her. "He seemed to like him well enough while Jeremy was working with us during the war." Suddenly, she doubted everything she believed about those months long ago.

Shirley shuffled over to the stove and put the kettle on for morning tea. "He thought you could do better. I guess that's why he hid them."

Ruth considered Shirley's suggestion. "Then why didn't he destroy them all? Why hide them? I mean, anyone could have found them and then..."

"Ruthie." Shirley came to the table and towered over her. "This was so long ago, dear. Whatever Dad's reasons were, they're long gone. You need to let this go. It's not worth getting upset about it now."

"But Shirley." Ruth clutched the letters tight to her chest. "I loved him."

Turning from the anguish in her sister's eyes, Shirley busied herself getting the teacups out and pouring them both a cup. Over her shoulder, she said, "Love is fleeting, Ruth. You remember how those other fellows were."

"I was waiting for Jeremy." Ruth hated the whine in her voice and coughed to clear her throat. "I knew something was wrong when Jeremy didn't come back."

"But all those other fine young men, you refused to give them the time of day."

"Were you jealous? Jealous they came to court me and not you?" Ruth rarely lashed out at her sister, but she was in pain.

"Dad needed me here, you know that." Shirley returned to the table with their cups jiggling against their saucers, and placed one in front of Ruth before sitting across from her. "I didn't have time for all that silliness." She still refused to meet her sister's eyes.

Ruth left her cup untouched. "I need to lie down for a bit." But she remained in place, her shoulders slumped.

"I'm sure you do, after all that pacing last night," Shirley answered tartly. She took a single sip of her tea, then bustled her nearly full cup back to the sink. "I'm sure you'll feel much better after a rest. Sara wants me to pick up some plants for the landscaping of her new tiny houses, so I might be a while. She wants me to spruce the place up before the magazine people come to do an article about her and her Tiny House Haven. I'm not hungry right now, so I'll pick something up on the road." She briskly rinsed out her cup and dried her hands as she watched her sister. "Oh, and the Mayor of Mountainview sent me another job offer. I'd even have a house to live in. But I refused it because I couldn't leave you alone." She patted Ruth on the shoulder as she passed, as if she were a child, then grabbed her purse and keys before walking out of the house. The door closed gently behind her, but Ruth stayed rooted to the spot.

She'd lived with Shirley her whole life. She knew when her sister was playing with the truth, and Shirley had just told a gigantic lie. Shirley's *tell* was the pat on her shoulder. Shirley wasn't a touchy-feely person. Even when their parents had died, Shirley had never sought comfort from anyone. But when she wanted you to believe an untruth, she patted you on the shoulder, as if to say, "There, there, I know better."

This pat spoke volumes.

Ruth was certain Shirley knew something about the letters, but how could she prove it? It wasn't like Shirley shared secrets with anyone.

Wait.

Shirley didn't have close friends, but she *did* have diaries.

Ruth had seen her writing in one the other night. Shirley had been adamant about her privacy when they were young, and had hidden them, terrified Ruth would read them and reveal all her thoughts and feelings. Or maybe laugh at her, which to Shirley would be even worse.

But Shirley didn't hide them anymore. She kept them labelled and preserved in boxes in the attic, pieces of ancient history that deserved to be treasured.

With renewed energy, Ruth decided to find them. A trapdoor in the ceiling off the hallway near Shirley's bedroom accessed the attic, a string pulling the ladder. A string that Ruth couldn't quite reach, even on tiptoe.

As she dragged a chair out of her bedroom and placed it beneath the access door, she knew what she was about to do at her age was fool hardy, maybe even dangerous. She knew it as she carefully climbed up on the chair and reached above her head for the string. And her inner voice shouted at her as she grabbed hold of the string and pulled until the hatch opened and the stepladder lowered with silent precision.

But she felt transformed, with a purpose, and suddenly full of energy.

Once she'd secured the ladder on the floor, and had the kitchen flashlight clenched tight, Ruth gripped the ladder rail with her free hand and took her first step. Then another. She could do this; she *would* do this. One step at a time, she rose toward the dark overhead opening.

A sharp crack rang out and Ruth caught herself by clutching tight to the ladder as the step beneath her left foot shifted. Dragging air noisily in and out of her lungs, she peered down to see the narrow step still attached on one side, but hanging by a thread on the other.

Up or down? Find the truth or let it go?

She glanced up; the attic entrance was within reach.

The truth—nothing but the truth would satisfy her now.

Shifting one step higher, wrapping her arm tight around the rail, she gripped the opening edge and climbed the last steps until she stood in the dark, overly warm attic. Her heart thumped inside her ribcage, bringing with it a warning pressure in the middle of her chest.

She hadn't taken her pills that morning, eaten breakfast, or gotten dressed.

She sneezed, once, twice, the dust thick on every surface.

Didn't matter.

Scraps of light flickered weakly through the few windows in the room, so she popped the flashlight on and swept the area with the powerful beam. They had never gotten around to installing a proper light here. It was for storage, not living.

Ruth shuffled from box to box, searching for the two with leftover wallpaper glued to the front. Shirley had tried to make them her own, fancying them up to hold her hopes and dreams in the notebooks she cherished.

Ruth found them towards the back, hidden under an old table, a white cloth across their top. A sliver of a faded scrap of the rose patterned wallpaper showed below, caught in the beam of her flashlight.

It took time, but she dragged the boxes from beneath the table and pulled the lid off the first one. The white labels with neatly written dates indicated they were more recent, the last forty years. Not what she needed today.

The second box held what she was looking for—tightly packed with Shirley's early diaries, beginning from when she had received her first one for her tenth birthday. Ruth pulled out a notebook with 1944 on the spine and took it with her. She left the boxes as they were on the floor, returned to the attic entrance, turned off her flashlight and gingerly climbed back down the ladder, avoiding the wonky step. It was a relief when she was back on solid ground again.

She left the ladder and her bedroom chair in the middle of the hallway. She didn't care if Shirley knew what she'd done.

When she finally eased herself onto the sofa in the living room, her breathing was shallow and her heart was pounding, but she *had* stopped first and taken her pills. The rain outside beat a steady rhythm on the porch roof, and she let the soothing sound settle over her body. And she waited. She waited for her medication to take effect, for her nerves to calm, for her mind to clear.

Then she opened the diary.

Chapter Two

Ellie McLellan hit save on her keyboard, then stretched out her achy shoulders. Another blog post written for her genealogy website completed and ready to go live. Between teaching her seniors group in person, and others through her website, about writing their own personal stories and searching for long-dead ancestors, she felt incredibly blessed to be doing what she loved.

She pushed back a clump of hair behind her ear and frowned. Something was being blown around by the rain and wind outside and making an awful racket. Cali, her four-year-old, golden-brown retriever, made it to the door before she did, and let out a high-pitched whine. "All right," Ellie calmed, pushing her aside, "we'll fix the noise."

She threw open the door to find a soaking Ruth on her doorstep. In the driving rain, Ruth's normally curly grey hair lay plastered straight against her head, her sodden dressing gown surrounding her fragile frame like plastic wrap. "Ruth!" Ellie pulled her in, slamming the door closed against the weather. "What happened?"

"He came back." Ruth struggled to talk through her chattering teeth.

"Hang on." Ellie guided her to a chair and gathered an armful of towels, which she wrapped around the older woman. "You can tell me all about it in a minute. Right now, out of these clothes, then I'll call Shirley."

"No." Ruth grabbed her by the arm and squeezed harder than a 92-year-old should be able to. Ellie looked at her in shock. Ruth croaked, "I don't want to see her."

"Okay, no problem." Ellie soothed her, taking a towel and wrapping it around her friend's dripping hair. She gathered Ruth's hands in hers and rubbed them briskly. "Let me get you some dry clothes and tea, and then we'll talk." She jumped up and set the kettle to boil. "I'll be right back," she assured Ruth, though the woman had not moved an inch. It was her dazed expression that worried Ellie. She asked gently, "Ruth?"

"Yes, yes," Ruth answered. "I won't go anywhere." She tried for a reassuring smile, but failed miserably.

When Ellie returned moments later with a pair of sweatpants, a T-shirt, zip-up hoodie, and a thick pair of colourfully striped socks, Ruth's expression had transformed from dazed to resolved. Her jaw was tight and her eyes were cold, sending a shiver of apprehension along Ellie's spine. Tentatively she asked, "What happened, Ruth?"

Ruth said, "If I see Shirley, I will kill her."

***

Ruth's shivering slowly stopped after she'd changed into the dry clothes and clutched a hot cup of tea between her hands. A few wayward shocks travelled through her body, but her teeth no longer clanked against the side of the cup, and her lips had shed their blue tinge. A packet of old letters sat on the table in front of her, drops of rain having blurred some of the handwriting on the top envelope.

Ellie waited for Ruth to explain what was going on. Their roles were now reversed, Ellie helping Ruth, when a few years earlier Ruth had helped Ellie through the loss of her family. Ellie and her late husband had bought this farm from Ruth and Shirley ten years before, when the sisters needed to downsize. This kitchen held memories for both of them. The old-fashioned counters remained unchanged, and the knobs on the cupboard doors were the same ones Ruth and her family had used decades before. Even the curtains above the sink were the same. This was a safe room for both of them.

Ruth let the cup rest on the table but kept her hands firmly around its warmth, and looked straight at Ellie. "How's your Aunt Jenna doing?"

The question threw Ellie. "Ah... Now that everything is out in the open, and Helen is getting to know Sophie, Aunt Jenna is doing really well." She hesitated, but Ruth nodded at her to continue. "And Sophie called this morning, and the doctors think Aunt Jenna will be home in a couple of weeks." Ellie paused. "But Aunt Jenna doesn't want to see me again until she's home."

"Good. You need the rest, but I'm glad you solved that mystery for them." Ruth gazed around the kitchen, as if soaking in the memories. "And your young man?"

"Well, he's not *my* young man." Ellie shook her head as if that action would make it so.

"After what you've both been through, I'd say he's your young man. Or could be, if you wanted. Saving his nephew's life is not a small thing."

"We'll see." Ellie hated talking about her personal life, and right now there were more important things to think about. "Now Ruth, please tell me what happened."

"Shirley hid the letters." Ruth pressed the damp bundle to her heart, her demeanour changing from thinking of others to the shock of what she had discovered.

Ellie hesitated, watching the pain cross Ruth's face and settle there as her shoulders curved forward, as if for protection.

"They were from a young man I was in love with. Jeremy." Ruth smiled tremulously when she said his name, and it made Ellie's heart break. "He worked here on our farm for a short time during the war, but signed up as soon as he could. He lied about his age; a lot of them did." Ruth sighed, and pulled the woolen blanket Ellie had placed there tighter around her body.

"What year was that?" Ellie asked.

"He signed up in December 1944 and shipped out early January. We had a last Christmas together here, and I never saw him again."

"Did he make it through the war?"

"I don't know." Ruth frowned at the thought. "But I wrote him every day. My father was none too keen on me spending the money on paper and stamps. We were barely hanging on, but I *think* he knew how much Jeremy meant to me."

"Jeremy must have appreciated all those letters."

"I had no idea until just now." Ruth gave a quick shake of her shoulders, as if shedding a terrible memory. "I didn't receive a single letter back from him. I waited each day for the post, but nothing came. It was a terrible time. I didn't know if he was still alive or... I *had* to believe he was alive. I lived on hope." She turned the letters over in her hand, still astonished to see her name and address on the front. "Shirley took them all and hid them. And she read each and every one of them!"

"Oh, Ruth," Ellie sat beside the older woman. Ruth couldn't contain the tears sliding down her cheeks onto the blanket, and Ellie took Ruth in her arms and held her until her friend calmed.

"He was coming back for me, Ellie," Ruth said, her eyes glistening with relief at the knowledge. "I had no idea what had happened. Was he dead? Maybe he didn't love me anymore? Why hadn't he written?" She rubbed her chest as if easing a deep pain and she struggled to breathe slower.

"Are you okay?"

"Yes, yes, it's all been such a shock."

"And what did Shirley say?" Ellie was furious one sister could do such a thing to another.

"At first, she said it was Dad who hid them, but I found her diaries. She told those diaries everything. If nothing else, I now understand her fear of being alone. I thought that was merely a silly grab for attention. When she hid Jeremy's letters, she was protecting herself, above everyone else. She stole my chance of a life with Jeremy, my chance of a family of my own."

"I can't imagine how that feels. What happens now?"

"I can't go back there, I truly can't. I'd do her some serious damage."

"Then you'll stay with me for as long as you want." Ellie patted her hand, then held it tight. "I haven't touched your old room. It was next on the list for renovation but..."

"You've handled your loss well," Ruth interrupted with some comfort of her own. "I never had a husband or children, but I don't think I would have your strength after losing them."

"And I have you to thank for that, Ruth. Do you remember how many times you found me in the treehouse at night?"

"It's a magical safe place. It was a favourite spot for Jeremy and I. You were strong, Ellie, full of hope and belief in the good of people."

A banging on the porch door drew their attention. Shirley was peering through the glass at them and her scowl did not bode well for anyone.

Ellie went to the door and held it open to allow Shirley inside, dreading the scene ahead. "Shirley, can I do something for you?"

"Ruth, you come home this instant!" Shirley ignored Ellie and headed straight to her sister, rain dripping off her coat onto the floor. Ellie got there before her and stepped between them, placing a hand firmly on Shirley's shoulder to stop any further advancement.

Ruth rose, the blanket falling to the floor. Anger simmered in her eyes, seeming to burn through every pore of her body. "You should be ashamed of yourself! I will never trust you again in my life!" She walked slowly out of the room, each step measured so she seemed in total control. Her shaking hands told another story.

Shirley moved as if to follow, but Ellie once again held her back. "That's not a good idea, Shirley."

"She's coming home, right now," Shirley blustered. "It's wet out and she could catch a cold. Or worse. You know she has a wonky heart, right?"

"I'm sure Ruth knows what's best for her. And right now, she doesn't want to be around you, and I think you know why."

"She *has* to talk to me." Shirley's bluster drained and her body hunched forward, as if the weight of what she had done all those years ago was finally coming to rest. "It was for the best."

"Best for who?" Ellie's question hung heavily in the air.

Shirley dropped her head and grabbed hold of the nearest chair before looking at Ellie with renewed belief in her eyes. "For all of us." She glanced once more through the door Ruth had exited, then left the house.

***

When Ruth returned to the living room after hearing the door slam, taillights of Shirley's car were fading down the road. "She's got some nerve!" Her voice quavered as if warring with her heart.

Ellie linked her arm through Ruth's. "We won't think or talk about her right now. Did you eat yet? And don't say you had a cup of tea because you know how I feel about breakfast!"

Ruth leaned into Ellie and let out a weary sigh. "Not yet, but I'm really not hungry. Just exhausted."

"How about I make you some toast and then you rest?" Ellie led her to the couch and made sure she had the blanket around her and pillows within reach. "Won't take a second. With food in your stomach, you can face any challenge."

"You sound like your mother." Ruth smiled at her. "She was extremely health conscious, you know. Would stop by to tell me the latest news she'd read about how to live to a hundred years old, what foods to eat, what to avoid."

"I know! She used to make these crazy recipes with what she called health food, but they tasted awful! Dad would always feed Mom's new meals to the dog. Poor Barney, he ate them all, but I don't think he liked them either."

"Then yes, I'll have a piece of toast, dear," Ruth said, pulling the blanket tighter around her waist. When Cali settled at her feet, Ruth gave her a quick pat.

Encouraged by Ruth's reply, Ellie pulled a piece of bread out of the fridge and popped it into the toaster. When it dinged ready, she lightly buttered it and cut it into soldier boys, just like her mother had done for her when she was ill. And she sensed Ruth was ill. Or at least her heart was broken in too many ways to count. And while slices of toast would not heal her heart, it might bring her some comfort.

But Ruth was asleep when she entered the living room. She'd stretched out on the couch, pillows piled under her head. The envelopes were clutched in her hands, the top one crumbled, its corners bent. Her hair had dried and relaxed once more into gentle curls that framed and softened the exhaustion on her face. Her feet, cozy in the borrowed striped socks, were sticking out at the end of the blanket, two oddly cheerful little soldiers, undoubtedly about to trod a new path in life. If Ruth was strong enough.

The thought made Ellie's heart ache. Placing the plate of toast on the end table, she tenderly rearranged the blanket so Ruth's feet were covered and her shoulders cocooned. She noted Ruth's even breathing, grateful for that, and wondered how she could help her friend through this upheaval.

Chapter Three

Ellie took Cali out for one of their daily walks around the farm. The rain had finally stopped, though it continued to drip from the trees as they passed beneath. Cali headed to the pond, her favourite spot on the entire property, and Ellie followed along slowly, worrying about Ruth back at the house.

Ruth had been a grounding force for Ellie when her parents had died in a car accident when she was twelve, and Aunt Jenna and Uncle William had taken her in. She loved growing up with her cousin, Sophie, finally having the sister she'd always wanted. Ruth was her teacher at the time, and she had helped Ellie through her grief.

And when Ellie's husband Adam and daughter Winnie had died via a texting driver, Ruth was by her side again, this time as a dear friend. Ellie wouldn't have gotten through the grief without Ruth's calm understanding and gentle guidance back into the land of the living.

Ellie popped into the barn to make sure all was well after the heavy rain. She and Adam had never kept horses here on the farm, converting the stalls into a play area for Winnie instead. One stall was outfitted with bunk beds where Winnie and her dad would spend nights camped out together. When her family had first passed, Ellie would come here daily, sometimes lying on the bunks to soak in their spirits. But now she came less frequently, usually to make sure the building was in good repair, though the memories still comforted her.

Cali barked in the distance and Ellie moved on to the pond where the dog sat still at its edge, fascinated by two ducks swimming calmly on the far side. The pond was big enough for swimming laps, but not for boats, and it suited her perfectly.

She snapped her fingers, and Cali came reluctantly to her side, still side-eyeing the ducks. Their walk continued through the forest, past the treehouse to the hidden highway entrance to the property. Ellie always checked it carefully to make sure it couldn't be seen from the road, and was satisfied it would keep snoopers from trespassing, but was still easy enough for Ruth to make her trips over to visit. The sun was breaking through the trees above, and birds were flying through the branches, chattering amongst themselves.

Twenty minutes later, the circuit they walked twice a day was complete, and she came back to find Ruth awake, crumbs littering the plate where the toasted soldier boys had been. That was a good sign.

Cali bounded to Ruth and lay her head gently in Ruth's lap, gazing at her with big brown eyes, begging for a head rub. As always, Ruth obliged. She smiled at the dog and plunged one slim hand deep into Cali's neck fur and rubbed it back and forth. "Who's a good girl?" she crooned. Cali obviously knew it was her because she gave Ruth a wet lick for her efforts.

"Cali, down," Ellie said. The dog ambled to the entrance and plopped on the floor, keeping all her favorite humans in full view.

Ruth said, "At first I wasn't sure Phil's gift of a puppy was a good idea, but Cali has been like a beacon of life for you through these years."

"A beacon and a storm at the same time." Ellie chuckled. She sat beside Ruth and stretched her legs out in front of her. "And I could make a coat from the fur she sheds."

"I'm glad Phil joined the genealogy group," Ruth said. "It took a lot of wheedling on my part to convince him. But then again, he's always been rather shy."

"I didn't think he'd come back after the first time," Ellie said. "And I'm not quite sure what caught his attention enough to return."

"I don't think it's a what, more like a who."

"Oh?"

Ruth refused to elaborate on her comment and they sat quietly for a few minutes.

"Ellie, I'll need a few items from home," Ruth said. "Some clothes, my medications, my eReader, perhaps my photo albums, and my Chantilly perfume. Jeremy gave me a bottle just like that for our only Christmas together. It reminds me of him."

"I'll go get whatever you need and make sure Shirley is okay."

"Oh, poo on Shirley!" Ruth muttered, shaking her head as if a fly was annoying her. "I'm sure she's just fine. She's stronger than she seems."

***

Empty bag in hand, Ellie knocked at Shirley's door ten minutes later, dreading the confrontation she knew was about to unfold. Shirley answered within seconds, as if she had been standing at the window waiting for someone to arrive. She didn't appear pleased that it was Ellie.

"Where's Ruth?" Shirley searched behind Ellie. "Why isn't she here?"

"She's not coming home yet, Shirley, but she asked me to get a few things for her for the night."

Shirley's eyes darted around nervously. "Fine." She moved aside and let Ellie into the hall. "Her room is at the back, on the right."

Ellie had been in the house before and knew her way around, but she took her time, not wanting to show Shirley how uncomfortable the entire situation was. Treat it like an everyday occurrence, don't get angry at the woman because she behaved horribly all those years ago. Get Ruth's things and leave. That was the mantra that played through Ellie's head, and she fully believed it would get her through this.

She hastily gathered the requested items and was about to make her escape when she realized she'd forgotten the Chantilly. She hurried back to the dresser and grabbed it. The memories Ruth had of that perfume were meaningful, and she wouldn't disappoint her.

Shirley was in the kitchen, her hands clasped and a worried expression on her face when Ellie walked in. "You know I can't cook, right? How will I survive if Ruth isn't here?" she jabbered, her voice rising. "I've never had to cook. I did all the outside work, the heavy lifting and such."

Ellie placed her bag on the table, opened the freezer and took out a frozen lunch. She peeled back the plastic and popped it into the microwave. "When it's time for lunch, hit this button four times to let it cook for four minutes. When it dings, take it out with oven mitts. Peel back the remaining plastic and check it before you eat. It could still be hot. Then wash the dishes." With that, she grabbed the bag and headed to the front door.

"But she'll be coming home tomorrow, right?" Shirley whined, trailing after her, almost frantic by the time Ellie stepped outside. "I mean, she can't stay with you forever. She has responsibilities here, and she can't hold a grudge after all these years."

"Why not?" Ellie asked quietly, staring at her until Shirley turned red and stepped back, her eyes glossing over.

Shirley pulled the screen door between them closed, but not before Ellie caught sight of tears spilling down her cheeks as she turned away.

"Oh, jeesh," Ellie whispered to herself, a wave of sadness engulfing her for each of the sisters.

***

An unfamiliar car was parked in front of the house when Ellie arrived home. And there were Ruth and Anna O'Brien, her daughter's teacher, sitting on the porch, chatting and laughing.

"Anna." Ellie climbed the stairs and hesitated a second before leaning into the open arms of Winnie's favourite teacher. "It's good to see you."

Ellie hadn't been in contact with many people since the accident, by her own choice. And she realized what a mistake that had been as she remembered all the help Anna had given Winnie through the years. The feeling of guilt took her by surprise, but it shouldn't have.

"Liar, Anna answered, pulling an elastic band out of her pocket and tying back her long blond hair, a sure sign this was not just a social call.

Ellie sat on the top step, and tried to catch Ruth's eye, sure she knew what was going on. But Ruth appeared to be fascinated by a blue jay in the large maple tree at the corner of the house. Conceding defeat, Ellie asked Anna, "What can I do for you?"

"Well." Anna rubbed her hands along her jeans, as if wiping off nervous palms. "I wanted to end the year with a fun activity for the kids. And since we're learning about communication in class, I was wondering if you'd give a lesson on how to interview relatives."

Ellie grabbed her chest, clumsily changing her reaction to a fumbling adjustment of her necklace. Blood pounded in her temples at the thought of walking into a class and confronting her daughter's friends. All those bright, young faces she knew, many of whom had visited her home, played in the treehouse, ran through the forest with Winnie.

All still alive while her Winnie was not.

Anna raised her hands as if to ward off any misunderstanding. "I think it would be really fun for them to ask their parents questions about what life was like when they were young. Most of us don't think of our parents as people having had lives, they're just... our parents."

"I think that's a wonderful idea," Ruth offered, her expression puzzled at seeing Ellie's reaction. "If you don't teach them about family history when they're young, when *do* you start?"

Ellie battled her fear. Deep breaths usually worked. She felt the heat ease from her skin as she forced her shoulders to uncurl from being almost bunched to her ears. If she thought of it like teaching the seniors at the Cozy Corner Café about genealogy, what would be the problem? She stole a glance at Ruth, part of her upset at her friend for corralling her into this, but how could she refuse?

Anna stood and gathered her purse. "I know this is short notice, but the idea came to me last night and I didn't want to wait another minute."

Ellie took another calming breath. "When would this be?" She already knew she had to accept.

"Next Thursday, around 9:30 in the morning, for about an hour." Anna hopped down the stairs to her car, probably in a bid to escape before Ellie could change her mind. "Call me if you've got any questions. It'll be fun." She climbed in, started the car, and waved as she drove off.

"Was this your idea?" Ellie asked.

"I wish it was." Ruth shook her head and smiled. "I can give you tips on how to handle an unruly bunch of ankle biters."

Ellie smiled slightly at Ruth's description. "I'll hold you to that."

"And how was Shirley?" Ruth asked, as if not wanting to know, but needing to.

Ellie held up the bag of Ruth's possessions. "She thinks you'll be home tomorrow, and doesn't understand why something that happened so long ago still causes you pain."

Ruth got up and took the bag from Ellie. "Shirley never was good at understanding emotions. At least not other people's."

"She's scared," Ellie said as she followed Ruth into the house.

"She doesn't know what scared is." Ruth headed to her bedroom but turned back. "She's always been in control of everything, or so she thinks. Sometimes it was just easier to let her think so and go along with it."

"That's no way to live, Ruth."

"No, it's not." Ruth continued on down the hall and spoke a bit louder. "And I don't intend to do that anymore."

Chapter Four

Ellie made them tomato, lettuce and cheese sandwiches in a bun for lunch, which Ruth devoured with lip-smacking glee. They ate on the balcony's glass table, on cushioned comfy chairs, with Cali stationed nearby, alert to any scrap that might fall her way. None did.

Ruth patted her mouth delicately with her napkin and sat back with a sigh. "That was just what the doctor ordered. Food always tastes better when you don't make it yourself." She pulled her pill case from a pocket, selected a tablet from its slot, popped it into her mouth and washed it down with swallows of water.

Cali sat up abruptly, ears twitching and a low growl surprising them. Ellie noticed the dark clouds moving in. "Rain's coming."

"Supposed to be a wallop of a thunderstorm this afternoon," Ruth said at the same moment a faint low rumble rolled across the sky.

Cali growled again and fled to the front door, waiting to be let in. Ellie gave her a quick reassuring pat, and opened the door to watch the dog disappear inside, probably to hide under the kitchen table. "She's not a fan of storms."

"Oh, but *I* am!" Ruth pulled her chair closer to the wall, well under the porch roof and off to the side to be completely dry should the winds pick up. "Don't mind me, you don't have to stay. I remember the big storm of September 1943. Jeremy and I got caught out at the treehouse and had to stay there for two hours until it passed. The noise was terrifying, and we were sure the tree would be struck."

"Why didn't you run for the house?"

"Oh..." Ruth smiled at the memory. "We decided it would be too dangerous to go running through the woods."

"But in a treehouse?"

"The time flew by." Ruth raised her eyebrows at Ellie and watched her grin as the answer finally hit her.

"I'm sure it did!"

"So often young people don't think of us older folks as having had lives." Ruth gathered her sweater around herself as the wind blew harder. "But I tell you, Ellie, it doesn't matter what generation you're from, teenagers are teenagers. He was my first."

And with that epic statement, the thunder boomed and lightning flashed across the sky. Within minutes they conceded defeat and ran for the house as the winds whipped sideways and no spot on the porch would keep them dry.

Ellie grabbed some towels and Ruth dried her damp hair quickly, laughing at the excitement of the storm, declaring, "Oh, this is such fun!" She fell onto the couch and pulled the now familiar cozy blanket around herself. "Come, sit, I want to show you this." She patted the seat beside her and waited for Ellie to sink into the cushions.

Ruth dragged her scrapbook from the coffee table and across her knees. As she opened the cover, another flash of lightning ripped through the house and lit the entire room. Ruth shifted the blanket from her legs, covering Ellie's as well. They were cocooned inside the house and under the blanket, safe and sound.

"I started this scrapbook a few years before Jeremy came into our lives," Ruth began, revealing a pencil drawing of a rose attached to the first page with yellowing tape.

"Wow," Ellie leaned forward and made out the intricate lines that formed the flower. "You drew this?"

"I did." Ruth beamed. "I started drawing as soon as I could hold a pencil. I rarely shared my pictures. The early ones were horrible. But it was something I had for myself. Something I didn't have to share with Shirley."

As she flipped the pages slowly, Ruth's talent became clear in the way a tree's branches arched to the sky, or a bird ruffled its feathers, or a young man's face grinned mischievously back at them.

"Is this?"

"This is my Jeremy," Ruth confirmed, running a hand lightly above the sketch, careful not to smudge the faded drawing. "I had no other picture of him until you had that copy made for me. I can't thank you enough for that."

"You're very welcome."

They glanced through the rest of the scrapbook as the storm outside abated, stopping at one intricate rendering of the treehouse from the inside. Ruth had captured every sliver of wood and each nail head that held the structure together. "The treehouse looks brand new!"

"It was about five years old at this point." Ruth tilted her head and stared off into the past. "Dad made it for us when we were in our early teens, actually. He thought we needed a space to hang out. But Shirley refused to climb the ladder; she didn't like heights. So, it became my haven."

Ellie stared intently at the sketch. "Wow, you even had a bed and a desk."

Ruth lowered her eyes, her cheeks blooming a shade of pink that was startling against her white hair. "Yes, well, it was my place, and I made it comfortable." She hesitated and then shared, "I drew this the day after Jeremy and I were together for the first and only time. It was a mild New Year's Eve. I had managed that summer to put covers over the windows, and Dad built the frame so well that the barest of cold air seeped through. Jeremy brought a few blankets, and we were snug as bugs in a rug."

"You're full of surprises." Ellie nudged Ruth's shoulder.

"Shirley came out trying to find us." Ruth frowned. "She hated being alone, even then. We didn't make a sound, so we knew we were safe. But she stood there calling our names for what seemed like hours. That night Jeremy promised he would come back for me. He told me he loved me with all his heart. His unit left three days later, and I never saw or heard from him again. I thought he had changed his mind. I thought..."

"Oh, Ruth, I'm so sorry." Ellie put her arm around Ruth and held her tight.

"A couple of weeks later I found out I was pregnant."

***

Ruth's revelation had exhausted her. Ellie assured her they could talk more later, if she wanted, and helped Ruth to her old room for a nap. She brushed aside Ruth's apologies for being such a burden, and left her tucked in and drifting off to sleep.

The rain had stopped, and the sun was slinking through the clouds when Ellie took Cali out to clear her head. She had never heard of Ruth having a child, and she wondered what had happened to it. Poor Ruth, what a terrible loss to go through at such a young age.

Ellie grabbed Cali's toy from the porch as they headed into the woods, and threw it ahead of them along the path. Cali ran, grabbed it and brought it back to her, then sat patiently in front, tail thumping. Ellie threw it again. And so it continued as they walked their familiar route, ending finally at the garden at the side of the house.

When she and Adam had bought the house from Ruth and Shirley, Ellie was sure she had found her paradise. She'd been raised in nearby Percyville and had often passed the Cotter farm on bike riding adventures. In those days, it seemed to be on the outskirts of town, but now the town had expanded around it.

Ruth had taught most people in the town of Percyville and the surrounding area at the local school. Once a year Ruth and Shirley, much to Shirley's discomfort, held an end of school year picnic for the graduating class. Ellie had fond memories of her own year's attendance here, because that's when her love for the farm had sunk deep into her bones.

All the kids had been on their best behavior, because Ruth was—well—Ruth. The best teacher, confidant, and towards the end of her career, grandmother to all. She was compassionate yet strong minded, expected good manners and hard work, and everyone tried their best. Even at an end-of-year party, when kids would normally get a bit wild, they wanted Ruth to be proud of them, so there wasn't much nonsense going on, but a lot of fun and wonderful memories.

Ellie had wandered away from the rest of her classmates that day, finding the treehouse but not trying the rickety ladder. Instead, she scrambled through the dense woods, discovered old animal paths and followed them along a creek, arriving at the back of the barn. She could hear her classmates having fun in the distance—heard their gasps as they dove into the cold pond, squeals as the boys sprayed the girls, and whoops of joy followed by spectacular splashes as braver students cannon-balled into the cold water.

She shook her old memories away and stepped into her barn for the second time that day, back in the present. Why she needed the comfort right now, she couldn't imagine. Perhaps not knowing how to help Ruth had drawn her back to take comfort from this place of happiness.

The cement floors were swept clean and the bunk beds on the far wall had been stripped of sheets and blankets years ago. There was a table against the wall under the window where Winnie had spent hours drawing the flowers she had picked during their daily walks. Ellie had taken all the sketches off the wall of the stall and brought them into the house for safekeeping. Ruth's drawings reminded her of her daughter's talent, and it relieved her to realize that the pain of her own loss was finally easing. Never gone, but manageable. These days a smile would come to her lips when she remembered her family, not a gut-wrenching moan of despair. At least not all the time.

Cali nudged Ellie's palm with a wet nose and brought her back to the present. She headed to the house and found Tess, one of her senior genealogy group, sitting on the porch with a bright-eyed and lively Ruth.

"Don't worry," Ruth said to Ellie with a tight smile. "I've told her all about the Shirley drama."

"What a woman!" Tess shook her head in amazement. "And I'm sorry I'm a bit early, but I was so excited to get started that I couldn't wait a minute longer!"

"I was just telling Tess how surprised I am Lennie would let her spend money on this," Ruth said.

"I'm not charging Tess," Ellie said. "I don't charge friends."

"Oh, but I don't mind paying the going rate," Tess assured her.

"Adam left me well taken care of," Ellie said quietly. "This farm is paid for, I'm debt free, and I make money with my books and genealogy business. I don't need much."

"You're very generous, Ellie," Ruth said.

"It's what I love to do. And when I see people's faces when I find information for them, well, that's payment enough."

"So, you've put together all the information for Tess?" Ruth asked Ellie.

"Heavens no," Tess laughed. "Can you see me letting someone else do all the work?"

Ruth shook her head at her friend and smiled. "Not for a minute!"

"I've got a plan laid out," Ellie said, "and we'll do it together. Let's all go inside."

"I want to get the hang of using the various genealogy platforms," Tess said. "So I can do other searches on my own."

"And what is Lennie doing while you're here with us?" Ruth asked.

"He'll be back in an hour," Tess said as she stepped inside. "The thought of being with all us gals gave him a chill."

"I doubt that!" Ruth said. "I bet he's got some sports show to watch."

"He's become an Australian footie fan." Tess set her purse on the table and took the seat Ellie motioned her toward. "I can't make heads nor tails out of it myself."

"It's hockey for me and nothing else," Ruth admitted.

"Same," Ellie agreed as she set her laptop, pen, and notebook on the table. "Throw in some Formula One racing and I'm happy as can be."

"Should I leave you two alone?" Ruth asked, heading towards the living room.

Tess beckoned Ruth to the table. "Come and join us, Ruth. We rarely get time alone together, and I'd love you to hear about the family story. Three heads are better than one."

Chapter Five

Ellie served them cups of tea in her mother's fine china, and an assortment of cookies from the Café before booting up her laptop.

Ruth sat back quietly, nibbling a chocolate chip cookie with delight, eager to watch Ellie perform her genealogical magic.

Ellie wiped the crumbs from her treat on a napkin. "What exactly are you hoping to find?" she asked Tess.

"Well." Tess stirred sugar into her tea and frowned. "My mother never spoke about her father much. Only that he ran a theatre in some small town, and died young. I'd like to know more about him, and where this theatre is located."

"Did your mom tell you anything else about him?" Ellie asked, hoping for a bit more information to start the search with.

"Sadly, no," Tess said. "It never crossed my mind how odd it was that she didn't talk about him. But now that you're teaching us how to write our own life stories, I realize my mother hardly *ever* spoke of him. She talked about her mother, and I've met my grandmother, and all my mother's siblings, but I never met my grandfather. Mom did say he was born out west, but I don't know where."

"So, was he alive for the 1901 census?"

"Definitely." Tess nodded. "Mom was the youngest and was around two at the time."

"Then let's see what we can find." Ellie moved her laptop towards Tess, and Ruth pulled her chair closer so she could view the screen too. "I'm using a site called Automated Genealogy for the 1901 Canadian census. And here," she pointed to the page on the screen, "it's separated into the provinces first. So, we'll pick Quebec, and the next screen shows all the districts. Which one should I choose?"

"We grew up here, so pick our district."

"Right, and which town?"

Tess sat back. "I'm not sure. I know they moved from one town to another, but I don't know the name of it."

"That's not a problem." Ellie pointed at the top left of the screen. "This is the surname search box. We can search all the towns at once this way. So, what's the family name?"

"Halbert," Tess said.

"Halbert?" Ruth asked. "Are you related to Joseph Halbert from Stanway?"

"Cousin," Tess said. "Passed away a few years back."

"Sorry to hear that. He raised the best pigs."

"He did indeed."

"And what's the first name?" Ellie interrupted their reminiscing.

"Did you find any Halberts?" Tess asked, surprised.

"Ten of them."

Tess looked at the entries and squinted. "There!" She touched the screen at the name Edward Halbert. "That's him."

"And now we open the page where he's listed." Ellie tapped a button and a page with names and ages appeared. She scrolled down until the name Edward Halbert was highlighted. "It gives his name. He's head of the household, married, and his date of birth is March 14, 1881."

"Wait a minute." Tess sat on the edge of her seat and studied the entry. "Who is this woman under his name? Maryanne Smith. It indicates she was part of his household. Is that correct?"

Ellie glanced at it and frowned. "It does. Hold on a second."

"And where are my grandmother, and mom, and Uncle Stan, and Aunty Maude?"

Ellie hit another button and the images split in two. "The part we were looking at, that's now on the bottom, is an index. This part above is the actual census return and has more information." She maneuvered the screen to highlight Edward Halbert once again, and there it was in black and white.

"Who the heck is Maryanne Smith?" Tess asked again.

"What does it say?" Ruth asked from her position on the side. She stretched her neck to see, but shook her head in defeat.

"There's only Edward Halbert and Maryanne Smith listed at this address," said Ellie. "They are both married, though it doesn't mean they are married to each other. She is about ten years younger than him and he's listed theatre manager as his occupation."

"Okay, so that *is* him," Tess said.

"Appears to be." Ellie said. "So, let's go back to the original index with all the Halbert names on it."

When the page filled the screen once more, Tess pointed to an entry further down. "There, that's my grandmother and her kids, and there's mom."

Ellie split the screen once again, showing Tess's grandmother and her children.

They both read the entry quietly, until Tess sat back in her seat, arms crossed over her chest. "It doesn't make sense. Why weren't they living together? It's the same town, Tenner Falls, but different addresses. Grandmother is noted as married but..."

"You never heard about this?" Ellie asked gently.

"Never." Tess frowned.

"What about this theatre?" Ruth asked. "Can you find any information about that?"

Ellie typed in the name of the town and the word "theatre" into the search engine, and peered at the hits that came up. "The Tenner Falls Theatre."

"How original!" Ruth frowned, as if the name confused her.

"What's this?" Tess pointed to an entry about the town itself.

"Should I read the whole thing or just scan it for you?" Ellie asked.

"Scan for now, if you don't mind," Tess said.

Ellie skimmed through the article and jerked in surprise halfway through.

"What?" Ruth sat forward as if expecting an interesting piece of information.

"Well," Ellie squinted at the screen to reread a passage. "Your grandfather left his job at the theatre before this article was published in... I think it says 1907."

"Why did he leave?" Tess asked.

"It suggests that he had some unethical dealings during his term as manager."

The women sat in silence, absorbing the news.

"Anything else?" Tess asked quietly.

"No." Ellie shook her head. "It mentions the new manager, but nothing more about your grandfather."

"What next?" Tess asked. "How do we find out more?"

"Let's check the 1911 census. We'll go back to the 1901 census, and see that column at the far right that says links? It has the number eleven in it, which means it links to the 1911 census. Let's open this and—oh, my."

"What? Show me." Tess nudged her glasses up her nose and focused on the screen. "He was a prisoner? Where is this?"

"It says he's in the county jail."

"Well now, *that's* interesting!" Ruth said.

"But why?" Tess asked. "What did he do?"

"The reason isn't mentioned, I'm afraid," Ellie said.

"Maybe something to do with that unethical behaviour with the theatre?" Ruth suggested.

"But my mom told me he died in 1907; this is five years later. This can't be my grandfather."

"The birthdates are the same, Tess, and it states that he's married."

"How do I find out what his crime was?"

"If you want me to, I could do some research on that later."

"Yes, please." Tess sat back, shaking her head in disbelief.

"There's something else I can try," Ellie mumbled, fingers flying across the keyboard until she hit enter and sat back. "I want to see if Ancestry has his death certificate."

"Mom said he died in Ontario, though," Tess said.

Ellie quickly reset her search request and stared at the screen. She found one entry that looked interesting and hit the link. "Edward Halbert, died in Hawk Station, which is right over the border between Quebec and Ontario, five minutes from where he worked at the theatre, half an hour from the county jail. And Hawk Station had a hospital. This says he died in 1920."

"What?" Tess sat straight in shock. "That's way later than—let me see this." She dragged her chair up and let Ellie enlarge the screen for her to see the death record. Tess motioned for Ellie to move the document so she could see the pertinent information, then grabbed Ellie's hand to stop her. "Oh, my goodness!"

Ruth edged over to see what all the commotion was about. "What? What?"

"The person who identified the body was my mother," Tess whispered.

"And she told you he had died years earlier," Ellie said. "There must have been a good reason."

"Perhaps." Tess sat back; her lips drawn in a straight line of anger. "But no one spoke of him except to say he had been dead for ages. They never talked about what kind of person he was, what he did, or where he went."

Ruth touched the document on the screen. "What does that say? Divorced?"

Ellie read it and nodded. "At the time of his death, he was divorced."

She slapped her knee in frustration. "I can't believe this!"

Ruth resumed her seat and leaned around Tess to ask Ellie. "What's the name of this town again?"

Ellie turned back and read it. "Tenner Falls."

A small smile crossed Ruth's face. "That's about forty minutes from here. Very small, but quaint. I saw a show there with Jeremy. And you didn't know that's where they lived?" she asked Tess.

"No, and I never asked any questions either."

“You’d be surprised how little people know about their close relatives,” Ellie told them.

“It’s only forty minutes away?” Tess looked at her friends and raised a questioning eyebrow.

"Sounds like a road trip to me!" Ruth said.

Chapter Six

"Just keep an eye on her," Ellie said into the phone when Ruth appeared in the kitchen an hour later. "Got to go, thanks." She hung up. "So, Tess called back, and we can do the road trip tomorrow if you'd like."

"Great. Poor Tess, she did seem rattled about what you found out about her family. Maybe it's not always wise to go rooting in the past. But that wasn't Tess now, was it?" Ruth took the placemats off the counter and set the table, taking cutlery out of a drawer along the way.

Ellie hesitated. She hated people butting into her life, and she tried not to do it to others, but this was different. Why? Because Ruth meant a lot to her. And by extension, so did Shirley. "I was asking Maggie to keep an eye on Shirley, drop by, make sure she has enough food, that's all."

"She's never cooked a meal in her life." Ruth frowned, a worried tone creeping into her voice. She glanced at the pot on the stove and took a deep whiff. "Is that what I think it is?"

Ellie stirred the beef stew. "I thought comfort food would be a great way to end the day."

"You always were one to look out for others, Ellie. Thank you." Ruth sat and glanced around the kitchen. "My mother taught me how to cook in this room, but Shirley never got the hang of it. She preferred to be outside, working with her hands. My gosh, how she hated housework."

Ellie brought their plates to the table, and they dug in. The silence interrupted only by Ruth's frequent "mmm" noises between bites. The quiet was soothing.

After her last mouthful, Ruth sat back. "Oh, I so needed that. Thank you."

"My pleasure." Ellie started to clear away the dishes and caught Ruth yawning.

"I think I'll have an early night." Ruth stood and pushed her chair in. "But I'd like to show you something first." She held her hand out to Ellie. "Come with me."

Ruth took her slowly upstairs, to the bedroom she'd occupied for most of her life, and stepped inside. The lowering sun was streaming gently through the window, patterned by the large maple tree outside, casting shadows across the walls.

Ellie had left Ruth's old room intact when she and Adam bought the house, except for Ruth's personal possessions. Ruth and Shirley had moved into a furnished house, leaving Ellie and her family their old furniture, save for the mementos and family heirlooms Ruth couldn't part with. Meanwhile, Shirley had marched out with two suitcases and a few boxes, and never looked back.

"Here, come see." Ruth led Ellie across the room to the open door of the closet, revealing a large empty space.

Ellie moved to Ruth's side, not sure what she was supposed to see. Ruth ran her fingers along the side of the doorjamb and stepped out of the way. "There, can you see them?"

Ellie hunkered down. Engraved on the wood were the initials R.C. x J.B., surrounded by a rough heart.

"Dad didn't seem to mind, but Shirley was furious. She thought I had no right to deface the family home."

"Jealous, was she?"

When Ruth frowned again, Ellie wondered, maybe Ruth's memories of those long-ago days were crowding her mind, and she was just now beginning to realize they actually presented a much different picture.

Ruth answered distractedly, "I hadn't thought of it that way, but I believe so, yes. I — I think I'll go to sleep now, if you don't mind."

"Not at all." Ellie knew from experience that sleep could be the best medicine. "Can I get you anything? Help you get changed or..."

Ruth leaned into Ellie for a deep hug. "You're like the daughter I never had, my dear," she whispered in Ellie's ear. "Letting me stay here, listening to an old woman's problems is plenty." She pulled back and gave Ellie a little shove. "Now off you go. I'm sure Cali's dying to go for a run or a swim."

"And Tess said that we can pick her up at nine in the morning, if that's not too early for you," Ellie suggested.

"That sounds lovely," Ruth said, giving Ellie the first full smile since she'd arrived at Ellie's doorstep that stormy night. "This should be interesting."

"And Quinn's coming the day after to take me to the Canada Day festivities."

"Oh, what fun!" Ruth's eyes sparkled with excitement. "I'm sure you'll have a lovely time."

Ellie knew Quinn had become a quick favorite of Ruth's, and Ruth wasn't above a little matchmaking, or at least throwing what she considered "two well-suited young people" together as much as possible. Ellie asked, "You'll come with us?"

Ruth hesitated.

Ellie could almost trace Ruth's mental path. Canada Day meant a community event, everyone out and about, having a good time, chatting and eating. Ruth loved community events. But this year it also meant she'd likely be seeing Shirley, as well as her friends. Was she willing to risk it?

Ruth finally said, "We'll see how I feel that morning, dear." She picked up her nightclothes and started to change.

Ellie took the hint and headed downstairs. She waited until she heard Ruth use the bathroom and return to her room before she left the house, Cali at her side.

***

Ruth watched them from her bedroom window, and rubbed her right hip. The rain made her arthritis bothersome, and she wasn't used to all these stairs anymore. How wonderful it must be to be Ellie, free to walk unaided and painless, with your whole life ahead of you. Even with Ellie's loss, the young woman could begin again.

Ruth felt her life was nearly over, the love of her life had come and gone.

Was there a second chance for *her*?

Chapter Seven

"I don't mind sitting in the back," Ruth assured Ellie when they reached the car. "I've got my pillows to prop me, and it's quite comfortable."

Ellie opened the door and held the pillows for Ruth while she settled herself in the back seat, and then passed them to her. "I still think you should sit in the front."

"And deprive Tess of seeing the sites as we drive into Tenner Falls? I think not." Ruth clicked on her seatbelt and arranged the pillows to her liking. "There! You can't get this kind of comfort in a high-priced car, that's for sure!"

Ellie shook her head and smiled. "Fair enough." She slipped into the driver's seat, and fastened her seatbelt. She caught Ruth's eyes in the rear-view mirror. "I think you're just as excited as Tess is."

"I must admit, it's been a while since I've been on an adventure, and I appreciate keeping my mind off other things right now. And I would love to see if the theatre is as I remember it." Ruth's smile disappeared, and Ellie hoped this road trip would indeed be a distraction from Ruth's problems with Shirley.

Ellie drove slowly along the driveway, then onto the highway. The older woman had been quiet at breakfast, eating her cereal slowly but finishing it all. At least her appetite was still there. "Did you speak to Shirley yet?" Ellie asked.

Ruth gazed out the window at the passing scenery, taking her time to answer. "No, and I don't intend to."

"She's probably worried about you."

"Let her be." Ruth plumped a pillow and leaned into it. "It's about time she thinks of someone other than herself."

They arrived at Tess's to find her waiting on the porch, her husband Lennie by her side. She was dressed in casual clothes, and held a smaller version of her usually large purse.

"My, my," Ruth said. "She's ready for business."

Tess made her way to the car while Lennie stood watching them, a slight frown on his face.

"Now you take it easy, Tess," he called to her. "Ellie, I'm counting on you to make sure she doesn't overdo it."

"You have my word, Lennie," Ellie assured him. "Ruth's in the back, and these women are my top priorities."

"Well." Lennie opened the front door. "Okay. Have fun, dear."

"I will," Tess called out to her husband's back as he stepped inside the house. When the door closed, she explained his abrupt departure, "There's a footie game on."

Once everyone settled in, Ellie pulled onto the road, and they were off.

"This is so exciting!" Tess said. She twisted as much as she could in her seat to speak to Ruth. "I'm so happy you could come, Ruth. It's been a long while since we did anything like this."

"Without our gatekeepers, you mean?" Ruth said.

"Oh, they're not that bad." Tess grinned. "They mean well."

"Hmmm," Ruth grumbled.

"I was thinking of taking some back roads to Tenner Falls," Ellie said. "I've checked out the route and it's an area I've never been to before."

"But you've lived here forever," Tess said. "I would think you've been down every dirt road and highway."

"So did I," Ellie laughed. "But I'll rectify that soon."

"I can't believe you haven't visited all the cemeteries in the province," Ruth said in disbelief.

"If we pass one on the way, I'll definitely make a note of it," Ellie assured them.

They passed the ride through the back roads with small talk, catching up on life, and admiring the scenery as they drove through a string of charming little towns. Cemeteries *were* noted.

"This is it," Ellie said as they came to a road sign that read Tenner Falls, population 472.

Ruth leaned forward to catch a glimpse of the town ahead. "It seemed much smaller when I was here."

"More buildings were built, and people moved closer over the years," Ellie said. "Where to first, Tess?"

Tess checked the paper in her hands. "I'd love to see where they lived, so Grandmother lived at 32 Harris Lane and Grandfather at 17 Pleasant Street. My map says that Harris Lane will be the first street coming up on the right."

Ellie slowed as they reached Harris Lane. They turned down a street with large trees and good-sized homes, each spaced apart to give the other privacy. The homes appeared to be about a hundred years old, and when they located the right house, they parked in front of it and stared. The lawn was meticulous, and the paint on the building sparkled as if recently renovated. A family of five could have lived here comfortably, the second story showing ample windows.

"It's lovely," Ruth said.

"It is indeed," Tess agreed. "Though I doubt it looked like this a hundred years ago. The neighborhood seems pleasant."

"And the other house?" Ellie asked.

Ruth glanced at her paper. "17 Pleasant Street, at the other end of the town."

Ellie drove them back to the main road. They passed a diner, a pharmacy, and a combination thrift store and bookshop. Ellie slowed and peeked in the window. Bookshops were her kryptonite. Beyond was a larger building with a quaint marquee that declared itself as Tenner Falls Theatre. Ellie stopped.

"Oh, no," Tess said. "Let's finish with the houses and then come back."

"Sounds good," Ellie said and continued on.

The other side of town was run-down. Not shabby, as it was obvious a lot of homes were in the midst of makeovers; but the buildings were worn.

Pleasant Street branched off at the end and held a handful of homes. Number seventeen was boarded shut.

"Of course, it's abandoned!" Tess shook her head, as if trying to set her thoughts straight. "It's as if Grandmother was light and on the side of good, and her home reflected it. But Grandfather was darker, and his home is like this."

"Tess," Ellie said, "a lot has happened in a hundred years. These buildings have changed hands, and who knows what the circumstances were then, and even now for the owners."

"But I get what you mean, Tess," Ruth said from the back seat. "It's easy to give the people and the homes tags, but they might not deserve them."

"True," Tess said. "Okay, let's go to the theatre and see what shape it's in."

Within minutes they pulled into the theatre's parking lot, empty save for one other car. The posters on the side of the building declared coming attractions and current showings.

"Well, it's still in use," Ruth said as she moved her pillows out of the way so she could get out. "That's a good sign."

After helping each other out, they leaned against the car and gazed at the theatre. "It's bigger than I remember," Ruth said. She focused on the neighboring buildings, tapped Tess on the arm, and pointed across the street. "See that building with the funny roof? That used to be an ice cream parlour. Looks like a regular home now. Jeremy bought me my first caramel swirl cone there after the dance."

Ellie headed towards the front of the theatre and the other ladies followed. Without realizing it, they had locked arms, neither sure whether to hold each other up, or simply for moral support.

"Look at this." Ellie pointed to the window poster advertising a blues band that Friday night. It was a local band that Ellie had been to see and quite enjoyed.

Tess peered through the window, holding a hand against her eyes to block out the sun's glare. "Oh!" She jerked back in surprise as a face appeared on the other side.

A middle-aged man waved at them and unlocked the door, opening it a crack and leaning out. "Hi there. Can I help you?"

Tess froze, so Ruth jumped in. "Yes, you can. This young lady," she motioned at Tess and they all smiled, "is searching for information about her grandfather, Edward Halbert, who managed this theatre back in 1901, or thereabouts."

"Well, I'm the manager now. Come in, come in." The man held the door open and let them all file past him. "We're not open at the moment, but I'd love to help any way I can." He peered at Ruth and grinned. "You're Ms. Cotter, right? I had you in grade 10 at Percyville High."

Ruth stepped forward and peered at him. "Bruce Campbell? I didn't recognize you with those glasses!"

"That's me! With a few extra pounds," he joked as he patted his belly. "It's so good to see you." He shook her hand gently as Ruth introduced him to the group.

"I'm not sure what I'm looking for, to be honest," Tess admitted, gazing around the lobby and taking in the décor.

"How about I give you a tour?" he asked.

"We don't want to take up your time," Tess said, even as she took a few steps towards the entrance to the auditorium.

"Not at all!" He reached the doors and held them open with a flourish so they could all pass through. "I love this theatre. I've been working here since high school."

"So, I suppose you know the history?" Ellie asked, running a hand along one of the red velvet seats that filled the room.

The theatre's layout consisted of a semi-circle of seats with two aisles leading from two doors. The stage in the front was large enough for a good-sized band, and the area directly in front was wide open, as if for dancing.

"I do indeed know the history of this amazing building." Bruce led them slowly down one of the aisles towards the stage, keeping an eye on the elderly ladies and matching their gait. "The theatre was built before 1900. There were a few renovations throughout the years, but in 1970 a new owner bought it and did a complete overhaul. Except," he paused, a delighted twinkle in his eyes, "they kept all the old architecture and layout. Basically, they upgraded the electricity and plumbing, cleaned everything till it gleamed, which included painting and repairing damaged areas. The theatre was closed for six months while they worked."

"And what was the theatre used for?" Ruth asked.

"Early on it was live performances, concerts, plays and such. Then when movies arrived, they adapted for that as well. That was a big bread winner for a while. We still have live performances each month and weekly movies. It's not as much a cash cow as it was, but the family who owns it refuses to sell or change its use. At least it pays for itself and upkeep."

"You're very lucky to have this piece of history," Tess said.

"What did you say your grandfather's name was?" he asked.

"Edward Halbert."

"Come with me." He beckoned them to follow him out of the auditorium and along a hall, past the food stand, into an office at the back.

"This is nice!" Ruth said. The room was bright, with a wooden desk facing the door, a couple of comfortable chairs, and one wall filled with filing cabinets. Sunlight streamed through two long vertical windows, filling the room with a warm glow. But the crowning glory were the posters that covered every inch of the exposed walls. Some were faded with old movie stars, and others were blinding with their newly printed brightness of upcoming events.

"During the renovations, they removed a wall to a closet and made this room bigger," Bruce said. "It was the only structural change they made, but they wanted the hub of the theatre to be a productive space."

He opened the bottom drawer of the desk and pulled out a large, dusty ledger. "I told the owners they should keep all the old files locked away, but they want it to be...what did they call it, in situ?"

"That means on site," Ruth said.

"Exactly. This was the first manager's book detailing all the daily goings on." He placed it on the desk and opened the cover. "See this?" He pointed to the name written under the word "Manager".

Tess leaned closer and squealed. "That's my grandfather!"

Ellie fumbled in her bag for her camera. "Can I take a picture?" she asked Bruce.

"Of course." He took a step away to allow her to snap a few photos.

Tess reached out to turn the fragile page and looked at Bruce. "May I?"

Bruce pulled out the chair from the desk for her to sit. "Take as long as you'd like."

While Tess settled into searching the ledger, Ruth walked around the room and stopped in front of an old poster. It showed a band and dancers. The Simon Fraser Band. Ellie came to her side. "Is this the band you and Jeremy went to?"

"It is." Ruth smiled at the memory. "It was the only time Jeremy and I went anywhere on the sly. I had to sneak back into the house that night, or should I say, morning. Shirley caught me, but I said I was out for a walk because I couldn't sleep. In my fancy clothes! And I'll never know why she didn't tell on me."

"You should ask her."

"I don't think so." Ruth shook her head vigorously. "I have no need to speak to her about that."

Tess rose from her seat and shut the ledger carefully. "It was great to read that. Even if most of it was lists of supplies and employee shifts."

Bruce put the book back in the desk drawer, and they made their way back to the lobby.

"Have you heard anything ... nefarious about my grandfather?" Tess asked softly.

"I'm not sure what you mean," Bruce frowned.

"We found a newspaper article that mentioned the manager had left due to unethical dealings?" Ellie asked.

He took some time to consider the question, but shook his head. "No, sorry. I never heard about that."

"It *was* a long time ago," Tess said, obviously disappointed not to garner any further information about her grandfather.

"Bruce," Ruth said, "do you remember the essay you wrote about being true to yourself?"

His eyes sprang open wide. "Yes, I do!"

"How did that work out?"

"He said yes. It took a while to get married, but we have a daughter who's turning ten next month, and we love her to bits!"

Ruth patted his arm. "I'm thrilled to hear that."

"Your lessons about having courage in your heart left a mark on me," he said.

"That lesson was off the top of my head actually, and I wouldn't have had it any other way," Ruth said.

"And it changed my life, Ms. Cotter."

"Then I'm glad I followed my gut."

"You always were ahead of your time, Ruth," Ellie said.

"And now it's time to head home. I'm pooped." With a quick handshake to Bruce, Ruth headed out the door.

"Thank you for your help, Bruce." Tess shook his hand. "I've learnt a lot about my family here in Tenner Falls."

Bruce held the door open for them. "Glad to be of assistance."

Ellie followed suit and shook his hand as well, gave him a smile, and followed the older women to the car. Within minutes they were heading home. Tess had found little of interest in the ledger, but Ellie had taken pictures of her grandfather's handwriting so she had something tangible that related to him.

The ride back was quiet as each of them were lost in their own thoughts, and tired from the excitement. Tess had a slight frown on her face. Ruth stared out the window, fingers tapping on her knee to a soundless tune, and Ellie stifled a yawn.

Chapter Eight

The sun was shining this Canada Day, unlike the many rain outs in the past. Ellie's hopes were high that Ruth would join her and Quinn at the town beach, where most of the festivities were being held.

Ruth woke in a good mood, ate a hearty breakfast, again licking her lips in delight at not having to cook, and then excused herself to go for a walk around the farm. Ellie marvelled at Ruth's love of walking. Every day at the Tiny House Haven Community where she lived, Ruth would walk the entire route around the lake, usually in the early morning hours to avoid the heat and chatty neighbours. She told Ellie it kept her fit and gave her time away from Shirley who, much to Ruth's annoyance, had taken to hovering in the past months.

Ellie watched her leave with Cali by her side, knowing that should anything happen to Ruth, Cali would dash back to get her. She understood the woman's need for solitude; she'd fought the same feelings since losing her family, and she recently found herself looking forward to mingling with other people. Not a lot, just once in a while. Everything in moderation, she reminded herself as she dressed for the fête. And dressy for Canada Day meant shorts and a flowered blouse, instead of her usual jeans and t-shirt. And no, it wasn't because Quinn was taking her.

Well, okay, maybe a bit.

The crunch of tires alerted her to his arrival, and the excited twitch in her stomach exasperated her. It didn't matter they'd known each other for only a short while; what mattered was they had saved each other in a time of crisis. A lot had happened between them in a brief period, and she felt safe with him, so she wouldn't question her gut too deeply.

She wore a delighted smile all the way down the stairs and out onto the porch. With hidden appreciation she watched him climb from his car. His shorts fit like a second skin and his pale blue shirt slid across well defined muscles when he stretched into the car for a basket.

He held it out when he saw her and grinned. "Snacks for the festivities!" His Scottish accent sent shivers across her spine.

"They feed us there, you know," she called back, hopping down the steps to give him a surprise kiss. His eye-crinkling grin assured her she'd made the right move. They were cautious around each other, both amazed by their quick attraction, which made them even more careful about diving in headfirst. He, still not believing she didn't cringe at his facial scar, and she, still pushing away her fear of loss.

We're adults, Ellie reminded herself, peeking beneath the checkered cloth, and adults can do what they want.

Quinn put the basket back in the car and looked around. "And where might the shaggy beast be?" As Ellie nodded her head towards the woods, she caught him checking her out from the corner of her eye. Her silly smiles might give her away today.

Cali had heard the car and her normal response would be to bound out of the forest and dash to Quinn for rubs and loving. But this time, she appeared at the head of the path, pacing herself to the woman beside her. Ruth waved at them, never breaking stride but continuing on her slow and steady pace.

"I was starting to worry," Ellie said when Ruth finally reached them and rested against Quinn's car.

Ruth rubbed Cali's head. "I had a delightful companion." Cali glanced from Ruth to Quinn. "Oh, go on with you, you silly girl. Get some more loving."

Cali raced to Quinn and sat with a thud at his feet.

"Sweet mother," Ellie whispered. "What have you done to my dog?"

Quinn reached into his pocket and brought out a treat. Cali's tail wagged and her bottom shimmied as she sat. With a raised eyebrow from Quinn, she calmed and waited. He held the treat out and kept eye contact with the dog. With a brief nod, Cali delicately licked it off his palm and swallowed it in one gulp. "Good girl!" Quinn knelt beside her and gave her a strong rub.

Ruth pushed away from the car. "I believe I would like to go to the festivities with you, if that's all right?"

Ellie gave her a hug. "We were hoping you'd come."

"I brought folding chairs for all of us," Quinn said.

"And we'll come home whenever you want," Ellie promised.

"Let me get my sweater and..."

Ellie dashed up the stairs before Ruth could move. "Got it, and I'll put Cali inside while you guys get in the car." Cali knew something was happening and refused to move. "Come on, Cali. You can't go to this." The dog padded slowly up the stairs; head hung in defeat.

By the time Quinn had settled Ruth in the front seat, belted and comfortable, Ellie was back with Ruth's sweater and she hopped into the back.

***

Following Ellie's directions, Quinn pulled into the community parking lot near the beach and found a spot amongst the packed crowd of cars. Ellie helped Ruth out and grabbed the basket of food while Quinn popped the trunk and removed three folding chairs and a beach umbrella.

Ellie noticed her neighbors' reactions as Quinn walked past; their eyes open wide in amazement, whispers of "That's Owen Walsh, the movie star," following him as he pretended not to hear. She knew he hated being an almost mirror image of his brother, but once people noticed the ragged scar that ran from his temple to the side of his mouth, they usually thought twice about who they assumed he was. He'd told her he was used to it, but she'd seen him tense up when meeting new people, never knowing their reaction, and ignoring the shock of some.

She'd never really paid attention to his scar; it was just a part of him. She noticed his humour, his gentleness, and his ability with small children and animals. The important things.

As they passed the food stalls around the entrance, people called out their hellos and waved to Ruth. She was always polite, responding with a return hello or more familiar, "How are the kids?" and waited for their answer before continuing on. Because of Ruth's popularity, it took longer than expected to reach the beach, but Quinn had gone on ahead and scoped out the best place for Ruth to relax and enjoy the goings on. By the time Ellie arrived with Ruth, Quinn was on a grassy rise in the middle of the beach, umbrella shading the chairs below. He waved them over, and Ellie guided Ruth around some kids tossing a beach ball back and forth.

"Hey, you hooligans," yelled Ellie's best friend, Maggie Williams, to the kids as she approached Ellie and Ruth. "Look around you, or take it into the water!"

"But the water's cold, Miss Williams," complained a teenage girl.

"Then why are you wearing your bathing suit?"

The girl tilted her head towards the boys playing, and smiled back at Maggie.

Ellie settled Ruth into a chair, made sure she had bottled water nearby, then reached out to Maggie for a big hug. She spied her cousin, Pete, behind Maggie, a silly grin on his face. As he continued to renovate Ellie's downstairs bathroom, he had worked up the courage to ask Maggie out, and told Ellie he couldn't believe his luck when Maggie agreed. Which was his downfall, as Ellie had kept him at her place longer than necessary, bolstering his self-confidence one minute, and threatening his well being if he didn't treat her best friend properly the next.

"I'm still waiting on some pieces for your bathroom. Sorry for the delay," Pete told her.

"You know it's not a rush, Pete, anytime," she said over Maggie's shoulder. "Ruth's staying for a bit, so it works out fine."

"I'm here," Maggie whispered into Ellie's ear during the hug. "I actually said yes, and I'm out in public with a guy!"

"Lucky you." Ellie pulled back and marvelled at the sparkle in Maggie's eyes. It had been a long time since Maggie had glowed like this. She deserved some happiness, and time off from running the Cozy Corner Café.

"And you." Maggie stole a quick glance at Quinn, now deep in conversation with Pete about renovations and carpentry, something Pete did for a living and Quinn was beginning to build a business doing.

Maggie and Ellie took the two extra chairs next to Ruth and watched the games on the beach. The guys sank onto the grass nearby, and Quinn took out bottles of iced tea and passed them around to everyone.

Children with painted faces paraded up and down the beach, while a group of high schoolers played a furious game of volleyball at the furthest end. Ellie looked from one end of the beach to the other, glad to see how many of the Percyville full-timers had shown up. Full-timers here used to mean old-timers, but more families were moving out of the city and settling in their rural town every year.

Tammi Wilden, the local busybody, walked over to Ruth and planted herself with feet apart, as if to begin a battle. She sputtered, "Shirley called me last night to ask how to boil an egg!" as if this was the most amazing event to happen in Percyville in years.

"Did you tell her?" Ruth asked, not giving Tammi the pleasure of any other information.

"Of course I did!" Tammi shook her head in disbelief. "Why didn't *you* tell her? Not that I minded."

Ruth looked Tammi in the eyes. "I wasn't there." And she left it at that. Tammi waited, hoping for more, but Ruth gazed back to the water where an energetic competition of "push off the log" was in full swing.

From their peripheral vision, Maggie and Ellie watched Tammi shift her stance, unsure of whether to ask another question. She finally got the hint and moved away. When Maggie leaned in to ask, Ellie shook her head, whispering, "Later" under her breath.

Francois Savard, the mayor of Percyville, strode out onto the sand with a megaphone in his hand, raised it and declared "The egg toss will begin in five minutes. Each team should place one member at the rise there." He pointed past where they sat. "And the other member should stand along the line drawn out to the water's edge. Five minutes everybody, and may the best team win!"

Quinn and Pete both stood up, placed their drinks beside Ruth's chair, and held out their hands for their respective dates. Maggie and Ellie shook their heads in unison and waved them off.

"Oh, no you don't." Quinn grabbed Ellie and set her on her feet in front of him. "I've never done this, and you can't deprive me of this annual ritual."

"Same," Pete muttered, reaching out and pulling Maggie to her feet.

"Fine," Ellie smiled mischievously, "but I'm partnered with Maggie, and you two are together. May the best team win!"

She grabbed Maggie's hand and they ran to their places along the lines volunteers had drawn in the sand. Quinn and Pete seemed shocked for a minute, exchanged a glance, shrugged, and took their places beside Ellie and Maggie, respectively.

"You are so going to lose," Ellie told Quinn with a laugh.

"And you are so going to look good with egg on your face," he replied.

Another volunteer walked along their line, handing each player an egg before scurrying away. The mayor stood above them on the grass and gave his last instructions. "We start at this point. At each toss, if you drop or break an egg, your team is out. Those left holding an intact egg will take one step back and we'll continue until one team is left standing. On your marks, get set, toss!"

The eggs flew, some high, some low, some reaching their mark, some splatting and breaking in the sand between the two lines. The first toss was the hardest as each team got used to the distance, and how to throw and catch properly.

Quinn had thrown well, and Pete had caught the egg with a small flip. Ellie had done this before, with Maggie, and their execution was flawless.

Of the twenty teams that lined up, the first throw eliminated five. Each remaining team took one step back and prepared for the next toss.

"Toss!" The mayor raised onto his toes, as excited as a little kid.

This time six teams were eliminated, and a lot of egg splatted on people's clothes, hair or shoes. With good-natured laughing, they walked off the field while the nine remaining teams spaced out along the line. The team members cautiously took the requisite step back, totally focused on their game.

Ellie could feel Quinn looking at her and refused to be distracted. She kept her eyes glued on Maggie, now further down the beach than they'd ever managed to successfully toss before. It was her turn to toss, and she ignored the handsome man to her side.

"You're very sexy when you concentrate," Quinn whispered to her.

"Toss!"

Ellie fumbled her throw, but Maggie dove for it and caught it before it broke on the ground. Pete was equally successful. Five more teams were out.

Another step back and four teams remained. Ellie focused. She *had* to catch this. She didn't believe Quinn had never played toss the egg before. His throws and catches seemed effortless.

"Toss!"

Maggie aimed straight at her, high enough to reach but low enough so the downward drop would not crack the egg in her hands.

But Quinn wasn't playing fair.

"I can't wait to get you in the barn later and..." he growled. The deep tone of his voice sent a delicious shiver through her.

She glanced over with widened eyes to find him staring at her.

Splat—their eggs made contact! Quinn's egg hit him square in the side of the head. Ellie's egg hit her chest, egg oozing across the front of her shirt.

The fourth team hadn't made the distance. Their egg lay whole but too far away to be caught.

"We win!" yelled a couple of teenagers, leaping in the air at the end, one boy holding their egg aloft for all to admire. The pair danced up and down the line, bowing theatrically to the cheering crowd.

Maggie and Pete came running over to Ellie and Quinn, laughing. Maggie handed out tissues to wipe off the egg. But Quinn was focused over Ellie's head towards Ruth, his expression abruptly serious. He took off running.

Ellie whirled to see what had caught his attention. Shirley stood over Ruth, wagging a finger at her. People nearby were glued to the drama between the sisters, one slouched in her chair and the other raising her voice. When Quinn reached the pair, he unceremoniously took Shirley's arm and gently but firmly pulled her away from Ruth. Speaking quietly and shaking his head, he walked Shirley towards the exit.

Chapter Nine

Ellie sprinted over to Ruth. "What happened? Are you okay?"

Ruth took a sip of her drink with a trembling hand, her eyes darting to where Quinn was escorting Shirley away.

"Ruth?" Ellie asked again. "Are you okay?"

Ruth held the bottle out, as if unsure what to do with it. It wobbled. Maggie took it and dropped it in the sand. "I'm fine," Ruth managed, taking a deep breath and forcing a smile. She was obviously refusing to glance at her neighbors and focused instead on Ellie. "Really, she caught me off guard."

"What did she want?" Maggie moved her chair in front of Ruth's, blocking out the view of people trying to glimpse Ruth as she battled to get her emotions in check.

"She's angry." Ruth pulled her sweater around her shoulders. Ellie leaned over and helped her put it on properly. "Thank you, dear." Ruth looked around, feeling strong enough to stare some gawkers down until they turned away. "She doesn't believe I should hold a grudge this long, or that she has done anything terribly wrong. She wants me to come back home because she's lonely."

"Of all the..." Maggie said.

"She has no right to make any demands." Ellie leaned into Ruth. "You can do as you please, with your life and your feelings."

"I can't go back there yet."

"If at all." Maggie shook her head in wonder that Ruth was even considering it.

Quinn returned and opened his basket. He passed the women sandwiches, set his and Pete's on a nearby picnic table, then knelt in front of Ruth. "Mrs. Wilson offered to take Shirley home. She'll be okay, so there's no need for you to worry."

Ruth gripped Quinn's shoulder. "You're a good man, and I thank you for helping us out."

"You remind me of my grandmother." His eyes crinkled as he smiled at the thought. "And I don't enjoy seeing anyone being bullied."

"Oh, she wasn't so much bullying as being scared and acting out, loudly." Ruth unwrapped her sandwich. "She doesn't know how to cook and she gets hangry when she's hungry."

"Not to worry about that either," Quinn said after sitting beside Pete. "Mrs. Wilson bought a few sandwiches and odds and ends for Shirley to take home, so she won't starve."

Ruth murmured to Ellie, "You've found a good one there."

"I don't have..." Ellie spluttered, suddenly nervous about people thinking she and Quinn were an item, and yet smiling as she gave the thought serious consideration. She stole a glance over at the guys and found Quinn staring at her. He smiled and winked, and she winked back. Okay. This could be entertaining.

After they finished lunch, Pete gathered all the garbage for tossing. "Well, this has been fun, but Mags and I have another engagement to attend." He sounded formal and shy, seemed to suddenly realize it, so stalked purposefully to the trash container.

Ellie's eyes widened as she mouthed "Mags?" to her friend and gave her a thumbs up behind Pete's retreating back. "It was great to see you guys, and you'll have to come for dinner soon."

Maggie raised an eyebrow in disbelief. "Dinner? As in a dinner *party*? *You* giving a dinner party?"

"No, just a few friends for supper," Ellie rushed to say, to cover the shock of what she had opened herself up to. She'd held no gathering of any kind since the death of her family, and the offer had flown from her mouth. "Nothing fancy. Not black tie or anything."

"Shame," Quinn said. "You'd look amazing dressed up. Not that you're not amazing right now," he added in a sputtering rush, relaxing when everyone laughed.

"I think it's more than time Ellie got dressed up and back in the groove, as you kids say," Ruth said.

Pete was back, his game face firmly in place. He held his hand out to Maggie and she took it.

Smiling, Ruth said, "Off you go, you two. Have a wonderful Canada Day, and thank you for your company."

"Anytime, Ruth." Maggie gave her a kiss on the cheek then waved goodbye. The pair left hand-in-hand. Watching them leave, it occurred to Ellie they were a perfect fit.

The events had quieted a bit, people were finishing their lunches, and some brave kids were back out in the water for a game of water polo. Some of the parents walked the beach, eyes peeled for the younger children wading near the water's edge.

"Would you mind terribly if we headed back, Ellie?" Ruth shivered slightly. "I think a nap would do me good right now."

"Of course not. It's been a wonderful time and I'm glad you came."

"You can always come back for the fireworks later." Ruth looked from one to the other.

"We'll see," Ellie mumbled, not committing herself to anything further.

"Something to think about," Quinn said. "I'll pack up and meet you at the car." He started by taking the umbrella down.

"Oh, Ruth," Ellie whispered to her friend, "what are you thinking?"

"Like he said, something to think about."

Ellie walked Ruth slowly back to the parking lot, stopping twice for hellos. No one asked Ruth about the incident with Shirley, probably because Ruth's solid gaze let people know her business was private, and everyone respected that.

Once settled in the car, belted, and heading out of the parking lot, Ruth turned to Quinn, "So, Mr. Walsh, tell me about yourself."

Quinn sat straighter in his seat, as if the answer to the question was more important than it seemed. "Well, I was a police officer in Scotland, but retired and come to help my grandmother. She didn't like idle hands any more than I, so I kept myself busy fixing whatever needed fixing around the house. And it's an old house, so there was a lot to fix. But I found I enjoy furniture making, so I'm trying to build a business at it."

Ruth nodded her approval. "I would have liked your grandmother."

"And she you." Quinn stole a glance at Ellie in the rear-view mirror and caught her grin.

"And you're able to build your furniture in your home, in Montreal?" Ruth asked.

"Well." He shifted slightly. "I started with some smaller pieces, like chairs for a table, headboards, whatever the client fancies, really. But my current project is extensive. A full kitchen set, table, chairs, sideboard. The client is furnishing his home in an old style with thick pieces, and sadly my garage space is not handling it well at all."

Ruth frowned, considering his problem, then spoke over her shoulder. "Ellie, dear, why don't you offer Quinn your barn to work in? It's certainly big enough for whatever he's making."

Ellie's eyes widened as Ruth put her on the spot. Quinn in her barn? Working there every day?

Quinn caught her wild-eyed expression because he immediately squashed the idea. "Oh, no, Ruth, I wouldn't dream of imposing on Ellie like that."

Ellie and Quinn caught each other's eyes again, both seeing the potential in Ruth's proposition, and the complications that could arise. But what about the positive aspects–seeing each other every day? They both liked the sound of that but were afraid to acknowledge it outright.

"Oh, tosh!" Ruth threw her hands up in frustration. "Start it part-time, like on probation. How long will your current project take?"

Quinn stumbled with his answer, maybe not sure whether to continue the conversation at all. "They want the table and chairs by Wednesday, and are considering a bedroom set, but that would take at least a few months."

Ellie hadn't said a word, but her mind raced like a computer program, going from pros and cons and back again. She surprised herself by sitting forward and saying, "Sure, why not?"

"Working with that huge space *would* make the process much easier," Quinn admitted, his tone guarded.

"Fine." Ruth clapped with delight as Quinn parked in front of the house. As Ruth left the car, she murmured, "Let him try it for this project. Charge him rent and see what happens."

"Can I check it out?" Quinn motioned to the barn, excitement written all over him, and when Ellie nodded, he dashed to the open doors and disappeared inside.

"What have I done?" Ellie said under her breath.

"Made the best decision of your life," Ruth replied, giving her arm a squeeze as they headed into the house.

Chapter Ten

Once Ruth retired for a nap, Ellie let Cali out, and the dog quickly faded into the barn. For the next hour Ellie idled around the house, tidying up, moving out into the garden, then ending up in the barn to retrieve Cali and see what Quinn was doing in there so long.

She stopped in the doorway and gazed at the picture in front of her. Quinn was sitting on a barrel near the back of the barn's open area, leaning on a wall, eyes closed. Cali was at his feet, head in paws as if asleep, but when Ellie arrived, her tail thumped gently across the cement floor.

The slight noise alerted Quinn, and he noticed her standing at the entrance. He rose slowly from his makeshift seat and walked toward her. "This is perfect." His tone was hushed, as if not wanting to disturb the peace of the barn. "Are you certain you want to do this? I'll need some of my larger machines, and they're noisy."

She laughed; all worries vanished by his eagerness to make sure she was okay with the situation. "I'm fine with that. Noise doesn't scare me. But there is one item I don't think you've considered."

Quinn squinted at her, unsure of what was coming.

Ellie pointed to Cali. "She may be underfoot. You can't be here and her not be around. Especially since you appear to be her new best friend."

Quinn gave Cali a deep rub around her ears. She leaned against him, totally melting into the experience. "I think we'll manage."

"I can see that." Ellie stepped inside and tried to see the barn through his eyes. "It is a good space. I've kept it clean, and sometimes leave the barn doors open to air it out."

"I'll need to lock those at night to keep my equipment safe." Quinn walked over and tested the doors, obviously pleased to find they rolled back and forth with ease. "Is that okay?"

"Not a problem." She stood next to him, enjoying the feel of his solid form beside her. His strength and calm reassured her that listening to her gut might be the way to go.

"And I'll pay you whatever you want for the space and time."

"No, I couldn't..."

"Then no deal." He shrugged his shoulders as if it wasn't even an option. "I'd like to keep my business on a business level."

Oh, so that's the problem. This was only business. Right. Okay. Good to know. I can do that, Ellie thought. "A hundred a week?"

"That's not enough."

"Then no deal," she parroted his words back to him and spun on her heel, snapping her fingers for Cali to follow before heading into the woods for a walk. Let him chew on that bit of business.

"I'll take it," he called after her. "Can I bring my stuff tomorrow?" All thoughts of the fireworks later that night were now thrown aside for the anticipation of future weeks being in close proximity.

She didn't turn but gave him a thumbs up and continued walking, not daring to swing around and reveal her huge grin. She heard his car leave before she stopped by the treehouse and leaned against the ladder. With a loud "Yes!" and accompanying fist pump to the air, she looked around at her forest and for the first time in a couple of years, felt home was a good place to be again.

***

After a light supper, Ellie and Ruth set themselves on the balcony swing, pillows cushioning them and a shared blanket across their legs against the evening breeze. Heads leaning back, they watched the stars flicker in the darkening sky. Cali lay stretched out full length at their feet, her deep sleep breathing coming out in light snuffly snores to add to the evening's music of crickets.

Ruth fussed with the blanket. "When I found out I was pregnant, I was overjoyed."

Ellie sat still, realizing Ruth was about to share a part of her life she had not spoken about for many decades, if ever. Ellie linked her fingers with Ruth's restless ones and held on.

"I didn't write Jeremy about the baby, but I told him how we could marry when he came back, and I would wait for him. I should have told him."

Ellie startled when the first of Ruth's tears hit her hands. But not a whimper came from the older woman.

"A few weeks later, I knew for sure I was pregnant. I didn't go to a doctor, but I had missed my period and I was ill each morning. I knew."

Ellie nodded in agreement, remembering her own morning sickness with Winnie. It had debilitated her until Adam had come home with a case of ginger ale that helped ease her nausea.

"I hadn't heard from Jeremy, and just assumed that's the way it went in the war. I knew back then letters took a long time getting back and forth." Ruth pulled a tissue from the cuff of her sleeve and dabbed at her face. "I'm sure I was two months pregnant when it happened." She paused, as if dreading speaking the words out loud.

It happened?

"That February morning was bitterly cold, and we had a cow about to give birth. Dad was worried there'd be a problem with the birth. I was in the stall with the cow and Dad had to turn the calf. It was nasty work. Shirley usually helped him, but that morning had complained of an upset stomach and told me I'd have to help Dad." Ruth gazed over at Ellie's rapt expression and shook her head. "I didn't want to believe she did it on purpose, but maybe she did. I didn't think anyone knew about my baby, but I was having trouble hiding my morning sickness. Maybe she figured it out and wanted attention herself."

"Were you feeling better by this time?"

"I was, actually." She nodded. "And more than willing to be there for Dad as he brought a new life into the world. I'd seen it before, so I knew what to expect. But gosh, it was so cold that morning, and the cow was in distress. Dad called me into the stall to calm her as best I could. It all happened so fast I don't know how I ended up on the ground."

"Oh, Ruth!" Ellie gasped, dreading what was coming next.

"I was in the wrong place at the wrong time. I got a hoof in the belly. Dad made me leave, more worried about me getting hurt than losing the calf at that point. Somehow, I made it into the bathroom."

They sat in silence for a few minutes.

"Shirley found me an hour later," Ruth whispered. "I lost the poor baby while sitting there. I told her everything. I begged her not to tell Dad, and she never did. You know what, Shirley took really good care of me for a few days. I'd never seen that side of her. She knew how much I loved Jeremy and she assured me I would have other children. But how she could throw out such a remark, I'll never know."

Ellie knew for a fact that Ruth had not had children. Nor a husband. Nor anything other than living with Shirley her whole life. What a terrible shame.

"But I didn't." Ruth let out a deep sigh. "I thought Jeremy didn't want me anymore. I hadn't written about the baby, wanting to wait to make sure I was good and truly along. Superstitious, I guess. Good thing in the end."

"Ruth," Ellie said slowly, "why would Shirley keep the letters from you?"

"She didn't want to be alone," Ruth spat out, a sudden rage overriding her sadness. "She had nothing in her life for herself and didn't want me to be happy." Her chest heaved and her jaw clenched. "She's a very selfish woman."

"A very sad woman," Ellie let slip, knowing she had no right to judge anyone. Still, her heart broke for what Ruth had lost.

"But I found something to fulfill my life." Ruth smiled through watery eyes as the flush of heated emotions dissipated. "I became a teacher and probably taught most of the municipality."

"It's not the same, though."

"No, it's not, but all of you were the only children I ever had." Ruth shifted in her seat, finding a more comfortable spot on the cushions, eyes fixed on the fireflies dancing on the far side of the porch railings. She picked at the blanket and finally looked at Ellie. "Can you help me, Ellie? Can you find him for me? Or at least figure out what happened to him?"

"I was so hoping you'd ask me!" Ellie jumped off the swing and returned seconds later with her laptop. She snuggled back under their shared blanket.

"Oh, my." The sight of the computer flustered Ruth. "Let's take this slow, if you don't mind."

"Of course," Ellie assured her, hitting the power button on the computer. In under a minute, she was on the Library and Archives Canada website. "Let's begin here. This is a site that'll tell us if Jeremy died during the war."

"I need to use the facilities." Ruth stood abruptly, the blanket falling to the porch floor. A chill washed over Ellie; her legs suddenly exposed to the evening breeze. Or was the chill more about what they were setting in motion?

Her movement awkward and graceless, Ruth disappeared into the house. She was back too fast to have used the bathroom except as a destination to give her time to gather herself, organize her thoughts, decide what she really wanted.

"We don't have to do this," Ellie said when Ruth returned to the swing.

"No, please do," Ruth whispered. "Go ahead."

With a few keystrokes, a couple of minutes, and digging deeper into the files, they learned Jeremy's name was not among those Canadians who had died in action in WWII.

"So, he's not dead." Ruth let out a gasp of relief.

"Well, it means that he didn't die during the war. So, we can work from the idea that he came back to Canada. If you want, we can try and get his war records and see if that holds any information." Ellie tabbed out of the site and shut the computer.

"Well." Ruth resumed her nervous picking at the blanket. "That's all I can handle right now. He might still be alive."

To ease the tension, Ellie said, "Did I ever tell you your history class was what got me interested in genealogy in the first place? How you showed us that the stories we hear could be wrong, and we should try to leave the truth for future generations? You were way ahead of your time. It wasn't only Bruce you left a mark on."

"My goodness." Ruth smiled at her. "That was merely a substitute class, a bit of fun."

"Maybe so, but you always had an interesting activity for us to do. You were the most hoped-for substitute teacher ever."

Ruth let out a deep sigh, patted Ellie's arm and pulled the blanket off her legs. "Thank you dear, I appreciate the kind words and lovely memories, but right now I need sleep more than a bee needs a flower."

Ellie stood to help her, but Ruth shooed her away and walked into the house, letting the screen door fasten gently behind her. Cali sat up and nudged Ellie's fingers with a wet nose.

"Yes, yes." She ruffled Cali's head. "Last walk of the night. Off you go." And with that command, Cali took off into the forest. Ellie grabbed her mega flashlight and followed.

Memories could be so melancholy, good and bad, twists and turns in a life. She hoped she could discover what Ruth needed to find.

Chapter Eleven

Ellie and Ruth walked into the Cozy Corner Café at ten the next morning to find the genealogy seniors waiting for them at the table in the back room. Ellie had started this group at Ruth's request, mainly to get some of Ruth's friends into a social setting while doing something fun. Ellie was teaching them how to write their own life stories, exactly what she did in her monthly column at the local newspaper, and her popular online blog. She had written a few books on the subject, and also worked with clients who wanted to delve back into their family histories. These seniors were curious and open to the process of learning, but most thought their lives were boring. They met twice a week, on whatever days suited them as a group, as everyone's schedule was flexible.

Ruth hesitated when she saw Shirley sitting in a seat closest to the front, her eagle eye on the front door, as if waiting for her sister to walk in. Ellie slowed beside Ruth, catching Shirley's eye and giving her a steely gaze, as if to warn her against saying anything disruptive.

Shirley never could take a hint, and intercepted them before they could enter the meeting room at the back. All eyes were on them. "Ruth, you look terrible. You're obviously not sleeping well, and you'll come home with me this instant." Shirley spoke loudly, the words carrying around the whole building.

Ruth flushed a bright pink. "I'm fine, thank you." She pushed past her sister and said her hellos to her friends, a smile on her face as her colour slowly returned to normal.

Having greeted the rest of the group, Ellie stood before them with a determined glint in her eye. She would not let Shirley's tactics get to them. "We're going to do things differently today. I'd like to set out a hypothetical scenario, and I want you to throw out ideas on how to go about finding information."

Phil Richards, usually the quietest of them all, raised his eyebrows, his attention piqued. "This sounds interesting. I'm tired of writing about myself."

"Then this will be right up your alley." Ellie took a seat, opened her notebook and pulled out a pen. "So, this is about finding someone who served in World War II, and whether they might still be alive."

Shirley gasped. All heads swung in her direction. She kept her eyes down and scribbled on her paper, as if paying attention and actively taking part.

"This gentleman had a sweetheart," Ellie continued, watching Shirley for further outbursts.

"Oh, this is a romance!" Tess said with delight, surprising her quiet and often grumpy husband, Lennie, who sat beside her. She was an ardent romance reader and could smell a heart-warming story a mile away.

"In a way," Ellie said. "Let's say the sweetheart was expecting letters, but never received them."

"Oh!" Tess said, stealing a glance at Ruth but trying to hide the connection she knew about.

"It might take a while, but they *would* get through," Lennie chimed in. "My older brother wrote a lot of letters and we received them all, but sometimes weeks later."

"Well, for whatever reason, this sweetheart believed her beau had changed his mind about her because she never received a single letter from him. And she wrote to him faithfully."

"Oh, this is so sad," sighed Doreen, a feisty grandmother who'd lost her husband, the love of her life for over several decades, a few years before.

"It's hypothetical," Shirley blurted. Again, everyone stared at her, some with eyebrows raised and side glances at each other.

"Years later," Ellie continued, "the sweetheart discovered something had happened to the letters, and indeed her beau had wanted *very much* to be with her."

"Please tell me there's a happy ending," Doreen begged.

"It's just a story, dear." Ruth struggled to hide her own pain.

"What I'd like you to think about," Ellie said, "and throw out any ideas at all, is how do we find out if this gentleman is still alive, and how would we go about finding him."

Shirley stood abruptly, her chair scraping loudly across the floor. "I'm sure you already know the answer. You don't need us for this." She thumped over to the counter and asked for a glass of water, even though there was a pitcher and glasses on the table. Maggie caught Ellie's eye before getting Shirley a glass. A shrug was all Ellie gave her.

Shirley remained at the counter, cradling her glass in her hands.

The meeting continued on without her. "Did he die during the war?" Phil asked.

"Let's see." Ellie opened her computer and clicked through to the government site. "There is a site that lists those who perished in the war." She and Ruth already knew the answer to this, but Ellie wanted to go through it again to keep Ruth's story as private as possible.

"But we have no name," said Lennie, warming to the mystery. "We need someone who served and lived so we can try this out properly. Use my brother's name. Michael Dickens."

Ellie grinned at him, enjoying how the group was getting into the swing. She took a quick look at Ruth and noticed her side-eyeing Shirley. Eyes down, Shirley reluctantly sat back at the table. "Michael Dickens. Let's see what happens when we put his name in." She typed, but the enquiry had no result, as expected.

"We need to see an entry of someone who did die." Phil said. "My cousin, John Richards, didn't make it home."

Ellie typed the name in and turned her computer around to show them the result. "So, this is a good way to start the search. In our story, we now know he didn't die in the war. He came home. What should we search for next?"

"Well, we don't know exactly what year he came back in," said Lennie. "He could have been injured and been evacuated early."

"I would say Facebook," said Phil, the newest techie in the group who had recently joined Facebook and reconnected there with family and friends. "But Facebook didn't exist back then."

"No," said Ellie, "but they may have joined later, like *you* did, Phil. So, we'll check out Facebook next." She jotted that note down. "But for this case, let's say he's not on Facebook."

"I know there are voter lists to about 1975, so he might be listed in those," piped up Doreen.

Ellie made a note of that as well. "That's a great idea. Let's use Lennie's brother as our example from now on and see what we find."

Ellie opened her Ancestry account and scrolled to the records for Canada and voter listings, then entered the name. "Bingo. Did he live in Montreal?"

"For a while, yes." Lennie looked at the screenshot and pointed at a few items. "There he is with his wife, Anna, in Mount Royal to be exact, in 1957. They moved to Ontario in 1960." He leaned closer to the screen. "His occupation was painter, and it even shows his address."

"Okay, this is great." Ellie gave them a glowing smile. "So, we've figured out to try Facebook, and voter lists. What else?"

"What about checking various obituaries to make sure he hasn't died between the war and now?" Ruth said, looking straight at Shirley. A staring contest began between them, each refusing to blink—until they noticed everyone's attention was firmly on their interaction, and abruptly broke it off. The group was too polite to ask questions, but they all knew Ruth was staying with Ellie, and the curiosity about what was happening between the sisters was straining their last shreds of decency not to ask why.

Ellie thumped her palm on the table and softened it with a forced laugh, knowing the noise would disrupt the growing tension. "That's a wonderful idea. So, let's assume we have an idea where he was living before he went to war, and the possibility he would return there afterwards."

"We can't assume that," Doreen said. "People came back and moved all over the country. So, you'd need to do a countrywide search."

Ellie beamed at her. "I'm glad you picked up on that."

"Can you search newspapers for obituaries?" asked Lennie.

"Of course," Ellie said. "Another good idea. You can Google newspaper archives and quite a few will turn up, some of them even free. Ancestry has a great collection as well. An interesting thing I've found is that you might find the person you are searching for referenced in another person's announcement, *like* an obituary, or a marriage announcement."

"I found the married name of a great-aunt that way!" Doreen said.

"Exactly!" Ellie nodded.

"But if they were sweethearts, wouldn't they have talked about their families?" asked Tess, reaching for her husband's hand on the table. "Maybe he talked about where he was born and raised. Maybe there's people still living there who remembered him or knew what happened to him."

"Unless he had no people," Ruth said quietly. "Maybe he was orphaned and had no other family left alive. He was alone."

"That would cause a problem," said Phil, deeply ensconced in the hypothetical aspect of the lesson. "But they still would have talked. Maybe he shared dreams with her, what he was hoping to do when he got back. Did he want to be a doctor, go to school, live in a certain place?"

"All good points, Phil," Ellie said. She noticed Ruth writing furiously in her notebook and smothered a smile. As much as Ruth wanted to move slowly in finding Jeremy, she was keen on figuring out how to do it.

"I wish this hadn't been just a lesson," sighed Tess, stealing a glance at Ruth. "I would love to find someone's long-lost sweetheart and there be a happy-ever-after ending."

"You're such a romantic." Her husband shook his head. "But I kinda agree."

"Happy-ever-afters don't exist," Shirley exclaimed. "Life is never fair, and one has to do what one has to do."

Ruth's head rose slowly from her writing and she drilled Shirley with a slit-eyed stare. "And sometimes, one has to have faith in those you love not to do something that would harm you." She snapped her notebook closed and stood. "Excuse me." She left the table and headed towards the restrooms, leaving the group quiet and frozen, sure they were witnessing the root of the problem between the sisters.

Ellie powered off her computer and gazed around the table. "So, does anyone have any questions about their own research?"

The silence was deafening.

Chapter Twelve

"They had a lot of wonderful suggestions," Ruth said from the passenger seat in Ellie's car on the way home from the meeting. "But what if finding out the whole truth is more painful?"

Ellie pulled off the highway and headed up her driveway. "We won't do anything you don't want to."

"You know, I'm really surprised how upset Shirley was that I wouldn't come home with her." Ruth knew she shouldn't feel good at the minor victory she'd had over her sister. "She'd never make a fuss in front of people, that's for sure."

"Ruth, what she did was unforgiveable." Ellie parked in front of the house and sat still. "But she's obviously suffering."

"Good." Ruth didn't move but stared out at the forest beyond. "In hindsight now, I see where she had a heavy hand, but there were also times when I let it happen, so I guess I'm also to blame." She turned to Ellie. "But *not* this. This is above and beyond. She knew how much Jeremy meant to me and I to him. It's pure jealousy, and I will never forgive her for keeping his letters from me."

She opened her door and with effort, scrambled out on her own and headed for the house, bypassing Ellie's outstretched hand. Ruth was coming to the realization she had always been on her own—she just hadn't realized it. Why should now be any different?

***

The sound of a truck coming towards the house had Ellie leaning out the kitchen window to catch a glimpse as she finished up the lunch dishes. Drying her hands quickly, she stepped out to see Quinn open the tailgate and check on the equipment strapped tightly inside.

He saw her on the porch and waved, his excitement evident. "These are most of the machines I need," he said as he grabbed a large workbench and pulled it towards him. "I'll bring the projects I'm working on tomorrow. For now, I want to set my tools up and figure out where all the equipment works best."

"Can I do something?" she asked, knowing she'd never be able to carry any of the pieces in the truck.

"You could grab the stuff on the passenger seat for me, thanks." Quinn pulled a dolly from inside the cab bed and plunked it on the ground before easing the bench over and onto it. Leaning the dolly back and making sure it was stable, he headed to the open door of the barn.

Ruth followed the goings on before settling herself onto the swing, giving Ellie a thumbs up as Ellie gathered some of the items from the front seat and followed Quinn into the barn.

The lights inside were on, even though the sun was streaming through the windows and the open doors. Ellie stopped to watch Quinn as he walked around the space with the dolly, stopping here, checking the light there, moving to another spot before finally settling on what he considered the perfect location. He maneuvered the work bench into place. It settled with a thump.

"This'll be great!" His enthusiasm was contagious, and she beamed back, holding out her armful of tools. He moved quickly and took them from her, still grinning like a kid in a candy shop.

"I'll get the last pieces."

"Wait." He touched her arm. "I can't thank you enough, Ellie. You might think me working here is a little thing, but it'll mean finishing this project on time, because now I've got the room to move around in and work properly."

"I'm thrilled I can help." Following his gaze around the space with her own, the place took on a different view. Once it had been the playhouse for her daughter, a sometime garage for her husband, but mostly just a building. To see someone excited to use it again made her happy. Suddenly the barn felt alive with potential.

They walked out together, Quinn pushing the dolly, and Ellie back to the front seat for another armload of extras. It took an hour and three more trips before all Quinn's equipment was in the barn and placed to his satisfaction.

***

Ruth studied them, noticing how well they worked together. She listened to the excitement in Quinn's voice as he explained various tools, and caught the twinkle of life in Ellie's eyes and delight in her voice as they joked back and forth. Cali sat at Ruth's side, knowing to stay out of the way of such activity. Absently, Ruth let her fingers run through the dog's fur and felt the comfort seep into her body.

***

Late afternoon found them all sitting on the porch with a beer for Quinn and lemonade for the ladies, a bowl of corn chips and a container of dip on the table between them.

"So, what rent are you charging for the barn?" Ruth asked as she carefully scooped some salsa onto a chip and popped it in her mouth. By her surprised and pleased expression, salsa was a new taste sensation. "It would be best to keep it businesslike," she continued, not looking at either of them, but her words were strong.

"I'd certainly feel better about it," Quinn agreed. He took a swig of beer to wash down some chips. "That way we can stop any time if it's not working for either of us. No hard feelings. I think you said $100 a week, but..."

Ellie tried to catch Ruth's eye, but the older woman was having none of that. Giving up, she said, "That's the number. I'll give you a month's grace period and if it goes well and you want to continue, you can back pay me."

When Quinn didn't respond, Ellie caught the glance that passed between him and Ruth.

Quinn said, "To be honest, a hundred a week is really cheap, and I feel I should pay more." He caught her opening her mouth to argue and held up a hand. "But I will accept your price and I agree to discuss it as we go on."

"Agreed." Ellie spat in her hand and leaned over to shake Quinn's. His eyebrows spiked upwards in surprise, but he spat into his own hand and accepted her shake.

Ruth stood up. "Now, if you'll excuse me, time for my walk."

"I'll be right with you." Ellie scrambled to join her.

"No, thank you." Ruth patted Ellie's shoulder, forcing her to stay seated. "I think I'd like a ramble on my own, and then maybe a nap before supper. These brief naps are doing me the world of good." She took hold of the railing and made her way slowly down the steps, Cali at her side.

Cali looked back at Ellie, and Ellie nodded for her to go with Ruth. The dog's tail wagged, and though she would normally bound off like a wild animal, she stayed at Ruth's side, matching her slow steps.

"She's amazing." Quinn wiped his hands on his jeans before catching Ellie's squint at the mess he was making on his pants. He grabbed his napkin to finish the job. He stood and stretched. "I brought one small piece to work on. Would you mind if I went over and..."

"By all means." Ellie made a shooing motion and watched him make his way to the barn. She leaned back in her chair, content with the day. Her lips curled up in delight when she heard him whistling.

Chapter Thirteen

Ruth arrived at the treehouse, slightly out of breath but pleased with herself for making it at all. The morning's events had exhausted her, and her mind was struggling to find a balance between her reality of life with Shirley, and her dreams of what might have been with Jeremy. She didn't want to disappear into a world of what ifs, but her super power of optimism kept popping up.

A log lay against the bottom of the treehouse, under the ladder where she used to sit when she was young. She settled onto the wood and leaned back against the trunk of the tree, letting out a worried breath she might end flat on the ground instead. Cali sat beside her, nesting her head in Ruth's lap, eager for some reassurance that all was well.

Ruth let her fingers curl into Cali's fur and rub unconsciously as she searched for, and found, the initials carved on the underside of the ladder. A place they had thought no one would find them. RC x JB. Jeremy's face when he determinedly carved their initials on his last night flooded her mind, and she closed her eyes to hold the memories tight.

He had wanted to leave her with a piece of him she could return to, day after day, run her fingers across and know he'd left it here for her. A connection across the thousands of miles that would separate them. And it had worked. She had come faithfully each day, rain or shine, to trace the letters and say a silent prayer to whoever was listening to keep her love safe. Her eyes sprung open in shock.

Perhaps her prayers should have included that he *return* home to her as well, because while he had survived the war, he had not come back to her.

Cali wandered off, sniffing out some wild animal that had passed this way hours before, but she never strayed out of sight. Her head popped up from time to time, checking on Ruth before slowly lowering it to continue her detective work of the enticing smells.

Ruth enjoyed the birds overhead, the sun dappling the leaves in the trees, and gave herself up to wondering what her life would have been like had she received Jeremy's letters. She sat up abruptly as realizations suddenly overwhelmed her. He had written her many letters, and from what he had written, he had obviously received hers, as he replied to many things she had spoken about. So why then had he never come to her when he returned home? Why had she not heard another word from him, ever?

Her heartbeat raced and she struggled to calm herself. Deep breaths. Think logically. There was something missing in the timeline of what happened.

She settled back, instead asking herself questions she hadn't thought of in years. If she had married Jeremy, would she have had a family of her own? Children, grandchildren? Would she have become a teacher? That alone made her hesitate. Teaching was one of the most profound experiences of her life. Becoming part of each child's life over the years filled her heart.

What would she have gained and what would she have lost?

And now, did she have the courage to go further and find out if Jeremy was still alive? The thought he'd changed his mind about her still had the power to send an ache through her soul. Contrary to what Shirley believed, Ruth hadn't stopped thinking of Jeremy as her life unfurled through the decades. He had been with her always, perhaps in a special place in her heart, but always there. His last letter to her had not been about coming home, but instead full of the war he was currently embroiled in. The only thing that made sense, was that he had changed his mind. Something had happened to change his mind about her.

She stood slowly, and in seconds Cali was by her side. She would keep these new thoughts to herself, and she refused to decide on any course of action yet. But she was definitely curious to find out what had happened to him. That didn't mean she had to see him, she told herself. Finding out where his life had taken him might be enough. It might be.

***

Ellie roasted a chicken with potatoes and garden vegetables for supper. Ruth set the table and held out a third set of utensils, giving Ellie a questioning look.

Ellie wiped her hands on the rose patterned apron handed down from her mother that she refused to throw away, threadbare though it was, and nodded yes to Ruth's unspoken question.

She turned the oven off and covered the dishes of food, then headed over to the barn. When she stepped inside, Quinn was intent on chiseling a small piece of wood, bent double over it, each stroke slow and even, inch-by-inch, as if any sudden move would break it in two.

She knocked on the door as he raised his chisel from the wood, catching him before he made another cut. He glanced up, startled, then smiled. He didn't hide the way his gaze admired her, and Ellie was suddenly aware of how he must see her, hair falling out of a ponytail, sleeves rolled up, apron on and slightly dirty. "So," she spoke louder than necessary, trying to bolster her self-conscious awkwardness. "There's a whole chicken and fixings in the kitchen if you'd like to stay for supper."

Quinn straightened in a shot, covering the piece he was working on with a cloth. "That sounds great. I'm starving. Give me a couple of minutes to put things away and lock up and I'll be right in."

She spun around and raced up the stairs to the house, letting the door slam behind her.

Ruth seemed surprised. "He's not interested?"

"Oh, no." Ellie took another plate from the cupboard, brought the food to the table, and moved everything from one place to the other. "He's closing up." She placed a pitcher of water on the table, then fumbled with the knot on her apron before removing it and hanging it on the hook by the stove. She brushed her hair back and made sure the oven was off.

She could feel Ruth's eyes on her, probably thinking she was a giggly girl again, and feeling sorry for her. But her feelings were more about being uncertain, second guessing every thought and action, even with a smidge of hope glowing deep inside.

Quinn gave a quick knock at the door before walking in and heading to the bathroom. "Give me a second to wash." He held his hands up awkwardly, to show he was following the proper etiquette.

Ruth was already seated when Quinn returned and waited for Ellie to take her seat. Once seated, Ellie motioned for the others to help themselves. "Oh," she blurted, flustered. "What would you all like to drink? Wine, beer, grape juice, water?" She pointed to the pitcher of water already before them. Gosh, she was pathetic, she thought, shaking her head at her nervousness.

"Water is fine," Ruth answered as she took a slim piece of chicken breast from the plate Quinn held out to her.

"Same," he answered, choosing a leg and placing the plate between him and Ellie.

"Right," she said to no one in particular. "Dig in."

"So, what have you been working on all afternoon?" Ruth asked Quinn.

"It's a surprise." He wiggled his eyebrows comically.

"Not part of the big kitchen order then?" Ellie asked.

"No. I'll get into that tomorrow. I'm working on another project. I want to see if it's viable. I'd like to produce smaller items on the side, and it's something fun and quirky."

"I can't wait to see what it is," Ruth said.

The supper passed quickly and quietly as Ruth's fatigue was clear, while Ellie and Quinn were still exploring their new circumstances and being cautious around each other. By the time the dishes were done, courtesy of Quinn, Ruth announced she was heading for bed.

"And I better be off as well." Quinn folded the washcloth and checked the clock above the sink. Cali came and sat at his feet, leaning against his leg and gazing up at him.

"I think she wants you to come for our last walk." Ellie wanted it too, but was willing to believe it was because of Cali.

"Sounds good, let's go." He motioned for them to precede him, and let the door latch quietly behind them as they stepped out onto the porch.

The stars slowly appeared, the sky barely holding light, and the night creatures were making themselves heard. Cali ran off the porch and into the woods while Quinn and Ellie followed behind.

Quinn took her hand in his, and she let him. They were quiet, enjoying the fresh air and deep moist smells of the woods. He squeezed her fingers, and she squeezed back. Just like teenagers. And that was perfectly fine with both of them. They walked in silence, enjoying the feel of another person nearby.

By the time they returned to the driveway and Quinn's car, full on dark had overtaken the sky and Cali was sitting beside them waiting to see what happened next.

"I can't thank you enough for letting me use your barn," Quinn said, maybe more formally than he'd intended. He swung their entwined hands back and forth, seemingly edgy.

"It'll be good to have company around again." She held his gaze, feeling excitingly brave to do so.

"How early can I get here? I don't want to wake you and Ruth."

"As early as you'd like. We're early risers."

The hand swinging stopped when Quinn pulled her toward him, lowering his head for a kiss, first hesitantly, gathering assurance when she didn't back away. Their arms found their way around each other, leaning in, resting together.

Cali's whine broke them apart with a shock. Ellie stepped back, a smile making apples of her cheeks. "Wow."

Quinn let out a whoosh of air and ran his hand through his hair. "Wow, is right." He slid his keys from his pocket and promptly dropped them on the ground. Ellie hid a goofy grin as he swooped to pick them up.

And then they both stepped forward for one last kiss.

"So, I'll see you tomorrow then." He slid into the driver's seat.

"Looks like it." Ellie walked backwards towards the porch.

Both kept their eyes glued to the other.

"Good night," they said in unison, and then laughed, the sudden seriousness of their actions shattered.

Ellie shook her head, waved at him and walked inside. She heard the car ease down the driveway.

Each could not get to sleep for hours that night. And it didn't matter.

Chapter Fourteen

Ellie dragged herself away from her notes when she heard Quinn pull up outside. She checked the clock above the sink. Seven thirty-five. No wonder her stomach was grumbling. Instead of making breakfast for Ruth and herself, she had buried her nose in the mind-map of ideas she'd been putting together on paper to help Ruth find Jeremy. When Ruth gave her the go ahead to do so, that is.

If Ruth gave her the go ahead.

Cali waited by the door, tail wagging, before Quinn knocked softly. "Come in," Ellie called as she gathered her papers and piled them on one corner of the table.

Quinn looked around and, not seeing Ruth, closed the door extra quietly.

"What's that smell?" Ellie perked up when she saw the large bag he was holding, and her nose crinkled at the amazing aromas wafting across the kitchen.

He held up the bag. "I come bearing Cozy Corner delights."

"But Maggie's not open yet," Ellie said, double checking the time.

"I took a quick drive by Ruth's. Shirley seems okay, she was out watering the plants. And Maggie was waiting when I passed the bakery. She has a scary sixth sense, that one does," he said.

"Oh, that smells wonderful," Ruth said as she walked into the room, closing the last button on her sweater.

Ellie was relieved to see that Ruth looked better this morning, more colour to her cheeks and a shine in her eyes. "It would appear my renter has brought breakfast."

Ruth caught sight of the mind-map Ellie was working on and spun it around so she could see it better. "Lots of questions," she murmured.

Quinn lay his paper bag on the counter. "Why don't you ladies sit and I'll get some plates."

"Oh, no," Ellie moved to take over. "I'll do that."

"Ellie, dear," Ruth scolded, pulling out a seat, the mind map in her hands as she continued to read it. "You don't have to do everything for everyone."

Ellie froze, feeling caught out by the need to make everyone comfortable in her home, and worrying about any negative response from Ruth as she read Ellie's notes.

"I suppose." She took a seat beside Ruth and picked at the skin around her thumbnail. A terrible habit she had started after the death of her parents when she was eleven.

Ruth covered her hand to stop her. "Tell me about this." She pushed the paper towards Ellie.

"Just some thoughts about how we can find Jeremy, using ideas from the group and some of my own suggestions." Ellie noticed Ruth shift slightly in her chair, as if the topic was uncomfortable. "Only when you're ready though."

"Ruth, how old was Jeremy when you met him?" Quinn threw out the question as he opened all the cupboard doors looking for plates. He found them in the last one, of course.

Ruth hesitated. "You know, I'm not sure. He'd wanted to join the war sooner, but they told him to come back when he was eighteen. That was the summer of '43."

Ellie watched from the corner of her eye as Quinn searched through all the drawers for cutlery. It pained her not to go over and do it herself. But he'd brought breakfast, and was intent on doing this, so she would let someone else help out, as Ruth suggested. But it felt unnatural to her core.

"And how did you two actually meet?" Quinn brought the plates and utensils to the table, then returned with the croissants and eclairs he'd laid out on a plate, and strawberries and blueberries in a bowl. Next came the coffee for himself and tea for the ladies in three Styrofoam cups. "Would you like this in a proper cup, Ruth?"

She smiled at him, delighted to be served dessert for breakfast. "This is fine, dear."

"Well, this is decadent." Ellie knew she'd pay for it later, but claimed an éclair and scooped a generous portion of fruit onto her plate, assuring herself she'd eat healthy the rest of the day.

Ruth took her time fixing her tea the way she liked it, obviously enjoying the ritual, though Ellie suspected she was stringing out the task while considering where to begin answering Quinn's question.

At last, she said, "Sometimes things just happen." She took a sip of tea and put a croissant on her plate. "One morning Dad said he needed another body on the farm for the spring planting. Ma had passed that winter and it was Shirley, Dad and I doing all the work." She took a small piece of croissant, closing her eyes to savour the buttery taste. "Maggie is such a talented baker."

"Pass my lips and straight to my hips," Ellie said, licking the icing off her fingers.

"They're perfect the way they are." Quinn caught himself and stuffed a large chunk of croissant in his mouth. Ellie stared at him in astonishment and knew he could feel her gaze, though he refused to return it. "So did your dad hire Jeremy?" Quinn asked, focusing his complete attention on taking a level spoonful of sugar and slowly stirring his coffee.

Ruth took pity on him. "Actually, *I* did. I'd gone into town that morning for supplies, and Shirley and Dad were organizing the fields." She took a sip of tea. "I was more the housekeeper and cook, and they did the outside and farming work. It suited us, and I guess that's where Shirley's love of gardening and landscaping came from."

Ellie stole a glance at Quinn and caught his eye before he looked away, a hint of pink creeping along his neck from his blunder moments before.

"So, I was paying for the groceries and I heard this deep voice asking Mr. Fine if there was any work in the area. Mr. Fine asked him why he wasn't overseas with the other boys, but the deep voice said they wouldn't take him until the next summer because he was too young." Ruth smiled at the memory. "I swear that was not the voice of a boy." She gave a little shiver and Ellie caught Quinn's eye this time and raised her eyebrows in delight at how Ruth's story was unfolding.

Ruth sat back, teacup in hand, lost in thought. "It was exactly like the movies. I turned the corner and there he was. He turned and saw me and I swear, the minute we locked eyes, that was it for both of us."

"That's so romantic," Ellie said.

"Had you never seen him before?" Quinn asked the practical question, whether ignoring the romance part of it on purpose, Ellie couldn't tell.

"I would have remembered him." Ruth put her cup on the table and pulled apart the last bit of croissant. "I brought him home in the truck. Dad had taught me to drive, but I was so nervous. Usually he or Shirley drove, but I had to do it that day. I think I hit every bump in the road on the way home."

"I've never seen you drive," Ellie said.

"I don't enjoy it, but Shirley does, so she does all the shopping. I'm a walker." Ruth finished her breakfast. "I tried to strike up a conversation with Jeremy in the truck, but he was too tired to talk. He'd gotten off the bus at the last stop, and had to walk fifteen miles to our town. Not a car passed him to give him a lift that day."

"That's a distance." Quinn finished his last bite.

Ruth paused, remembering. "Dad took to Jeremy right away. He had good manners, was willing to learn, and he was strong. We had one cow in the barn, and a chicken coop out past the garden, so we fixed a space for Jeremy in one of the empty stalls. He loved it, said the cow's breathing at night was soothing."

"So, Jeremy used the stall Winnie and Adam used for their camp outs?" Ellie asked.

"The same one." Ruth nodded. "Dad and Jeremy fixed the toilet area in a couple of days, and he even had a barrel for bathing. He used the pond in the warmer weather. Dad didn't want Jeremy in the house for personal things like that, not with his two daughters there."

"He didn't trust Jeremy?" Quinn asked.

"No, I think it was more the way Shirley acted around Jeremy."

Ellie sputtered out some tea at the thought. "Shirley?"

"She was moon-eyed over him." Ruth tucked a strand of hair around her ear. "I don't know who I felt sorrier for, Shirley acting so outrageously, or Jeremy being so kind in his efforts to not hurt her feelings. He didn't feel the same for her."

"That must have been interesting." Ellie could not imagine staid and proper Shirley flirting with anyone. "Didn't it bother you?"

"I knew it wouldn't last, and it didn't. Shirley got the hint and didn't hold it against him. Until he showed interest in me."

A knock on the door startled them all. Ellie stood, wondering who would be calling on them so early in the morning.

Shirley stood there, scowling, waiting to be invited inside.

Ellie opened the door wide and let her in. Quinn gathered the dishes and washed them quickly. Ruth met her sister head on. "What do you want?"

"I'd like to talk to you, Ruth." Shirley was pale, a slight sheen of perspiration covering her forehead. When she couldn't seem to find what to do with her hands, she jammed them deep into the pockets of her sweater.

"Go ahead."

"Alone, if you don't mind." Shirley looked pointedly at Ellie and Quinn.

"I've got some unloading to do." Quinn set the dishtowel back on the hook and walked past them to the door. "Call me if you need me."

"Ellie stays," Ruth told her sister, daring Shirley to argue.

"Can we sit down?" Shirley walked slowly to the table and waited for Ruth and Ellie to sit before joining them. The silence was unsettling until Ruth started drumming her fingers on the table. Ellie remembered Ruth using that trick when her students were getting unruly. A simple drumming of the fingers, over and over, until the rhythm caught everyone's attention.

"Ellie and I have things to do, Shirley," Ruth said. "Is this going to take long?"

"When did you become so snappy?" Shirley shifted in her seat.

Ruth's stare was the only answer she got.

"Right. Fair enough. I need to tell you something, and I know you'll never forgive me for this, and I don't expect you to, but you need to know."

"How could there be *anything* worse than what you already did?" Ruth asked.

Shirley hesitated. She hung her head and said softly, "He came to the house after the war."

Ruth tilted her head, as if moving her ear nearer to Shirley would clarify the words. "What do you mean he *came* to the house? When?"

"You were at Mrs. Fine's place that afternoon, helping her pickle. Remember that? You came home with burnt fingertips because..."

"What do you mean he *came* to the house?" Ruth's voice was louder, and her posture upright and still.

Shirley found the courage to hold her sister's eye. "He came looking for you."

"I knew there was something else going on! But why didn't he stay? Why didn't you tell him I'd be back in a few hours, or send him to Mrs. Fine's?"

The anguish on Shirley's face made Ellie's heart break. The woman seemed to battle the future of her own life with her next words. "Because I told him you had married and moved away."

"Oh, Shirley!" Ellie blurted, unable to believe a sister would do such a thing. She had never had a blood sister, but she and her cousin, Sophie, had each other's backs through thick and thin, anger and love.

"I'm so sorry," Shirley whispered. "I'm so very sorry, Ruthie."

Ruth sat like a statue as she processed what Shirley had done to her, to her and Jeremy. She let out a gasp, a hand clutching her chest, her breathing coming fast and in great gulps.

Ellie ran to her, holding Ruth around the shoulders as she turned white and her body slumped. "Quinn!" she yelled. "Quinn! Come quick!"

Within seconds Quinn's footsteps pounded across the porch, and he was in the room. He didn't hesitate when he saw the situation, and gathered Ruth in his arms. "Get the keys, open the truck, we're going to the hospital."

While Quinn headed out the door with Ruth cradled to his chest, Ellie pulled Shirley from her chair and pushed her out the front door, locking it behind her.

"I'll call you when we know something." She left Shirley on the porch before jumping into the backseat of the truck to hold Ruth against her, protecting her from the jarring of the truck as Quinn sped down the drive.

She glanced back to see Shirley standing in the driveway, head down, alone.

Chapter Fifteen

Ellie shouted out directions for Quinn as they raced along the highway towards the hospital, Ruth held tight in her arms. Quinn squealed to a stop five minutes later in front of the small emergency entrance.

"Can they handle this?" he asked.

"I'm not dead," Ruth said as her breathing evened out. "It was just a shock."

Ellie unlatched the door, kicked it ajar, then struggled to help Ruth out. "It won't hurt for you to be checked out." She eased across the back seat with Ruth, then supported her as she sat upright.

Quinn left the car where it was, doors agape, grabbed a wheelchair from the emergency entrance and raced it back to Ellie and Ruth. "Here, sit." He eased Ruth onto the chair, then headed towards the emergency desk at top speed.

The nurse looked up in surprise. Quinn's eyes were a tad wild with fear, his scar standing out against his pale skin. Ellie stopped beside him, wiping sweat from her forehead, resting one hand on Ruth's shoulder.

"Please, Clara," Ellie said to the nurse, "she's had quite a shock. She grabbed her chest, and she's having trouble breathing."

Before Ellie's frightened prattling had stopped, the nurse shot out of her seat and dashed around the desk, kneeling before Ruth. She took out her stethoscope and placed it on Ruth's chest, listening intently. "There now, Ms. Cotter, we'll get you taken care of right away."

"I'll go move the car," Quinn murmured to Ellie. "I'll be right back." He hustled outside.

Ruth remained quiet, taking in the scene around her in the waiting room. Ellie could see, as always, Ruth's concern was more for others than herself. A young boy who sat beside his mother, cradling his arm, and a woman holding a bucket in front of her, her face green with nausea.

Ruth protested, "Clara, surely you can look after them first. I'm fine." This last declaration came out as a short gasp.

"Right," Clara rose quickly and spoke to Ellie. "I'm taking her in for tests. Her heart sounds remarkably steady, but we'll just make sure. It'll take some time, so how about I call you when we're done?"

"I'll stay." Ellie scanned the waiting room and chose a seat from where she could monitor the doors to the inner sanctum.

"I'm in excellent hands with Clara." Ruth gave her a brave wave. "You remember how good she was at science? She's a wiz."

"I remember how she tutored me through the last year." Ellie shot Clara a smile. "I wouldn't have passed without her. Off you go then." Clara winked and whisked Ruth off behind the doors for the ER doctor to examine her.

Ellie let out a deep breath and fell into a seat, startled when Quinn sat beside her. "You don't need to stay, Quinn. This may be a small hospital, but it's a good one and I know most of the staff. They're all great. I'll wait here, but you need to get on with that project." His frown told her she wasn't fooling him with her positive babbling. She was terrified for Ruth.

He hesitated, then stood and wavered. "Can I at least get you anything before I go?"

"Thanks, no. I'll use the time to stroll the halls and get a coffee or something." She gave him what she hoped was an "in control of the situation and not overly worried" smile. But she could tell he wasn't buying it.

He leaned into her and kissed her soundly before whispering. "I'll be here in five if you need me."

She reached up and ran her fingers into the hair at the back of his head, pulling him close for another kiss. It was crazy, but she felt his strength flood into her body. It gave her a sense of calm. "I'll hold you to that."

The waiting room crowd of three watched them intently. Any distraction from their own current situation was welcome.

Quinn headed out the door. Ellie felt suddenly alone without his presence near by, then noticed the curious glances from the people around her.

"Was that Owen Walsh?" The woman who held the bucket asked, her colour slowly improving. Maybe she was already thinking of the stories she could share about being in the same room with the movie star.

"Nope. He gets that all the time." She turned away, not wanting to explain Quinn was Owen Walsh's younger brother. And she desperately hoped nobody recognized her from the news reports of a month ago when she had been involved with the whole family.

Instead, she revisited what had happened in her kitchen that morning, wondering if she could have protected Ruth in some way, or at least lessened the blow. Ruth's memories, and Shirley's stunning and brutal revelation of what she had done, was unbelievable. Ellie shook her head, as if the physical act could erase the anguish that had fallen across Ruth when the reality of the situation had struck home.

And now Ruth was in emergency, possibly fighting for her life.

***

Ellie hadn't moved from her seat when Clara came over to her an hour later. "She's going to be fine. Dr. Eastman said she's a horse–okay, he said that behind her back—but she's really strong."

"We knew that." Ellie let out a whoosh of breath and smiled back at her friend. "Thanks Clara, I was so worried."

"We're keeping her for a couple of hours, hooked up to monitors. She's not happy about that, but you can go in and sit with her if you'd like."

Ellie stood, frowning. "I thought you said she was okay?"

Clara shook her head. "Hospital rules. She's ninety-two, for goodness sake! She takes half the medications other people her age are prescribed, and I don't doubt that'll be reduced before too long because she's doing so well."

"She walks, all the time," Ellie told her, stretching her back.

"That helps." Clara stepped behind her desk and motioned for Ellie to head back to see Ruth. "Honestly, Ellie, she'll be fine."

Ellie pushed through the doors and found Ruth lying in a bed in a curtained area of the emergency room, her fingers tapping on the blanket covering her while she stared at the ceiling. Seeing Ellie, she announced, "Did you know that there are twenty-four squares in each tile of the ceiling, except the one directly over me? How is that possible?"

Ellie laughed as she sat. "Trust you to notice something like that, Ruth."

"It's annoying is what it is."

When Ruth struggled to sit, Ellie gently guided her back. "No, Ruth, maybe you should wait for the doctor to do that." She leaned her arms on the bed beside the woman, welcoming the relief that coursed through her body. "We'll call Quinn soon enough and head home."

Dr. Eastman came over, took one look at Ruth's annoyed face and pushed the button to raise the bed. "Sorry about that, Ms. Cotter, you're good to be propped up."

"David," Ruth said in her serious teacher's voice. "I'm quite all right. I had some unexpected news, and it took me by surprise."

"Ms. Cotter," he countered in his serious doctor's voice. "I know you're all right, but there are rules to be followed. You drummed it into us that rules are there for a reason." He'd stumped her with her own teachings, and she had no comeback.

"Fair enough," she muttered as she made herself comfortable in the raised bed. Her eyes fluttered with exhaustion, and Dr. Eastman motioned for Ellie to follow him as Ruth fought to stay awake.

In the hall, away from the room, Dr. Eastman hesitated. "She's fine, really. The breathing problem was the result of the shock she received. Her heart's normal and regulated, and all the tests are clear. I'll be back in an hour and she should be able to go home." He searched the hall. "Where's Shirley? I've never seen them apart."

"Well," Ellie said, not sure how much of Ruth's private life she should reveal.

"Sister squabble? Is that what caused this upset?"

"I think so, but I was so scared for Ruth."

"Ellie." He squeezed her shoulder, already stepping away to go to the next patient. "You did right to get her here so quickly. Try not to let her get too excited for a bit. She'll be fine. We can't lose a treasure like Ms. Cotter. But I'd check in on Shirley if you can. She has more serious medical issues than her sister, and I'm not sure she's told Ruth about them."

"Oh?"

"Can't say more," Dr. Eastman said as he walked away. "But promise you'll monitor Shirley as well."

She wondered how Ruth would manage over the next few days, now that she knew what Shirley had done. Not to mention finding out Shirley had been concealing her own medical problems. Ellie pulled out her phone to let Shirley know Ruth was okay. It was not a call she wanted to make.

***

Quinn drove them home midafternoon. They arrived at the house with sun streaming through the trees and birds chirping to each other as they darted through the branches. Quinn helped Ruth out and up the stairs of the porch where Ellie waited, having flown up the steps to open the door.

"I let Shirley know you're okay, but she said if you don't call her yourself, she's coming over. But first, I think a bite to eat would be in order."

"Fine," Ruth muttered.

Ellie reached out to take Ruth's arm, but Ruth shook her head, letting her know she fully intended to manage on her own.

"A small sandwich would be nice, then I'll take a nap." Ruth let out a yawn and quickly covered her mouth. "I can't seem to stay awake!"

Quinn pulled a stack of sandwiches from the fridge and placed them on the table, then got some glasses and juice. Ellie shook her head in relief that she didn't have to make them herself. She was suffering from worry and exhaustion herself at the moment, and a nap later sounded perfect. But right now, nothing this man did would surprise her. "Awesome," was all she said, joining Ruth at the table.

Quinn sat across from them and shrugged. "I figured we'd all need to eat at this point."

"How is your project coming along?" Ruth asked before taking a delicate nibble followed immediately by a larger bite, apparently finding the ham and cheese sandwich to her liking. "I'm sorry I've caused a ruckus and taken up your time."

"Actually, Ruth." Quinn waited to finish chewing before continuing. "When I got back to the barn, I caught a miscalculated measurement, so it saved me a lot of extra work by not having to fix it."

"Sometimes there's a silver lining," Ellie mumbled. "Gosh, these are good, Quinn. What's your secret?" She pulled the bread apart and tried to figure out what he had put into it.

"I'll never tell." He grinned at her and jammed the last quarter of his sandwich into his mouth before standing, chewing faster than anyone Ellie had ever seen. "Sorry to leave you ladies, but work calls."

"Thank you for this." Ellie waved at the plate of sandwiches.

He took another big one to go. "My pleasure." He bent and gave Ruth a hug, whispering in her ear, "You had us worried." Then he left, Cali by his side.

Ruth's shoulders slumped the moment he was out of the house, and she let out a tiny gasp of breath.

"Ruth!"

Ruth waved her away. "No, no, I'm fine. Just worn-out, and I hate being a bother to anyone."

Ellie hesitated. "Do you want me to call Shirley and tell her you'll call later?"

There was no response for the longest time, then Ruth finally answered, a determined glint in her eyes. "No. I'll do it now, *then* take a nap. I'll call from the bedroom." She left the room slowly, obviously not relishing what lay ahead.

Chapter Sixteen

The phone receiver weighed heavy in Ruth's hand as she sat on the bed, waiting for her strength to return. The anger and disappointment that had walked into the room with her had seeped away. She was alone with her fears of what lay ahead, how her life would change, how Shirley would react, and whether she had the strength to stand up to her.

She dialled her own number and jumped when Shirley answered on the first ring. Had she been waiting nearby all this time?

"Yes? Yes?" Shirley's tone was brisk, tinged with a wisp of exhaustion. "Ruth?"

The last thing in the world Ruth wanted was to start this conversation. The mere thought of it had her finger poised above the button to disconnect before saying a word. "I'm okay, Shirley."

"What happened?" Ruth could hear her sister pulling a chair across the floor to sit by the old phone still attached to the wall. It was an old original Percyville house they lived in now, two old women with old technology, yet it suited them. "Was it your heart? Are you still in the hospital? Do you want me to come and get you?"

Ruth held up a protesting hand Shirley could not see, wanting to stop the flow of anxious words invading the calm of her bedroom. "I said I'm okay. The doctor told me to rest, no stress, you know, the normal stuff they tell us old folks. I'm still at Ellie's."

"Hmm," Shirley let out a breath. "So, when are you coming home?"

"I don't know." The silence between them made it abundantly obvious that they would not solve the problems overnight or through one phone conversation.

"I know I shouldn't have kept the letters, Ruthie." Ruth could tell Shirley was winding herself up to tell her what she thought Ruth wanted to hear. "But it was for the..."

"Don't say another word, Shirley Geraldine Cotter!" Ruth exploded. "Not one word. I can't forgive what you did. It was the worst thing a sister could do. Jeremy and I were going to be married."

"How do you know that for sure?" Shirley started her usual dance of misdirection. "He left you when you were pregnant. He didn't even mention it in any of his letters! How could you possibly believe a life with a man like that would be worthy of you?"

Ruth sucked in a shocked breath. "That's below you."

"All I'm saying is you never know what would have happened."

"And *you* made sure I never had the chance to find out." Ruth waited, daring her sister to produce some nonsense to defend herself.

"When I found you in the bathroom, bleeding, your face white as chalk," Shirley whispered. "Ruthie, I thought you were dying! When you told me he had left, I thought it was *because* of the baby."

"I never told him about the baby. He *never* knew!" Silence filled the air between them before she continued, fighting for calm. "I know you've always been afraid of being alone. Me marrying Jeremy would not have changed that. But I never would have left you to fend for yourself. Never!" She smacked the bed, failing miserably at retaining her cool.

"Would have?" Shirley's voice was small and quiet, breathless, hearing Ruth's use of the past tense. "And now?"

"I have a lot of thinking to do, Shirley," Ruth muttered. "Jeremy may still be alive, and I want to see him, ask him to forgive what happened."

"You mean forgive me."

"He thinks *I* didn't wait for him. You told him I *married* someone else," Ruth enunciated each word slowly, as if explaining to someone who didn't understand, for obviously her sister had no clue what this would look like to Jeremy. "He doesn't know it was all you."

"And if you find him, what will you do?"

"I don't know." Ruth stared out the window at the trees in the forest beyond, each blowing in the wind, surrounded by other trees, entwined beneath the ground. Roots. Shirley was her remaining blood roots, and she wasn't sure how to proceed. "But I've a lot of thinking to do."

"So, when will you be home?" There was a definite whine in Shirley's voice, a touch of fear, but still thinking only of herself.

"When—and if—I'm ready," Ruth replied before hanging up.

***

Ellie spent the next couple of hours working on a project for a client, fixing supper, and taking a long walk with Cali, who had become Quinn's sidekick and was reluctant to leave his side even for their regular walk.

When Quinn arrived in the kitchen for supper, Ruth was already at the table, and Ellie was setting out the last dishes. After quickly washing, he made himself comfortable across from Ruth. "This smells amazing." He eyed the pasta dish, salad, and warm rolls as if he hadn't eaten in days.

"Help yourself." Ellie motioned to the food, and spooned out some salad for herself and Ruth.

"How are you feeling, Ruth?" Quinn asked. "Did you manage to sleep with all my noise?"

"Oh, I can sleep through anything these days." Ruth took a bun and a pat of butter. "Especially with the bedroom on the other side of the house. And thank you, I'm much better. I called Shirley to let her know I was fine, then basically hung up on her. It was surprisingly satisfying."

As Ruth made no more mention of Shirley's visit and declaration, the topic was not brought up again. They spent the meal discussing Quinn's creations and his plans for the future.

"I've been thinking, Quinn," Ruth said during a lull, "you should stay overnight while you're working on this project."

Ellie choked on her drink and Quinn moved to pat her on the back. She raised her hand to let him know she was fine.

"I mean, the stall is still there with bunks," Ruth continued, seemingly unaware of the glances between Ellie and Quinn. "There's a bathroom and..."

"You know what," Ellie declared, nodding her head in agreement, "that would be a great idea. You can use the shower in the house, and I'll provide meals."

"Well, that raises the rental fee." Quinn pretended to be grouchy.

"And well worth it, young man," Ruth assured him. "Think of the extra time you'll gain to create your marvelous pieces."

"Then that's settled." Ellie rose and started clearing the dishes. When Quinn moved to grab the dishcloth, she shook her head. "Not tonight. Off you go. Tomorrow's another day."

"Thanks for this, Ellie. Let me know when it's time for Cali's last walk and I'll go with you, then head home."

"And bring lots of clothes tomorrow," Ruth interjected. "Pretend you're going camping for a couple of weeks."

Quinn headed out the door, Cali on his heels, and the room was quiet except for the tinkling of dishes in the sink.

Ruth said, "It'll be nice having someone around."

Ellie caught her smiling at her. "Wait a minute, are you matchmaking?"

Ruth left the table and pulled on her sweater. "I don't think there's any need for that. You two seem to be managing just fine. I'm going for my walk and then I'll curl up with a book, if you don't mind."

Ellie stopped her from leaving, pulling the woman into a gentle hug. "As long as you're okay, that's all that matters to me."

"We will talk about it, Ellie, but not right now. My mind is overflowing with things."

"When you're ready, I'm here."

Ruth pushed a stray strand of Ellie's hair behind her ear, patted her cheek, and headed out the door.

Ellie jumped at the sudden hammering from the barn. What had she agreed to? The arrangement with Quinn sounded good, and maybe it was exactly what she needed – to have someone around. And it didn't hurt he was interested.

***

Ellie arrived at the barn as the sun was setting. When Quinn caught sight of her, he quickly covered a piece of work with a cloth, straightened and stretched. "Have I thanked you for this?" He motioned to the space in the barn.

She stepped inside and stroked Cali's head when the dog came to rest against her. "Many times. And I must say I'm impressed with the set up." Ellie walked around, noting the placement of large machines, the makeshift workbench along one wall covered in his tools, and the clean floor, broom and wood debris all swept into a far corner. "I'll get you a garbage can."

"Thanks." He checked the time, then arranged his tools neatly on the bench. Switching off the lights, he followed her out, pulled the doors closed, and snapped a brand-new lock on the clasp. "I hope you don't mind this, but the tools are expensive." He handed her an extra key.

She pocketed the key and shook her head. "Good idea."

They headed into the woods together, Cali bounding ahead of them, checking back occasionally as if unsure about this new nightly routine. Their fingers found the other's as they strolled through the trees. The night was heavy with humidity; a storm was predicted for the deep night hours.

"I could get used to this," he said softly.

She stole a glance at him in the darkening light, and felt a giddy excitement course through her. She was letting herself believe a relationship could develop with Quinn, and it scared and thrilled her at the same time. "Me too."

She knew she was on what he considered to be his ugly side, the side where a scar ran from his eyebrow to the edge of his mouth, courtesy of a bust gone wrong while working as a police officer in Scotland. The scar was old, but a brilliant doctor had sewn it to leave a slight puckering. Some people saw only that, but she rarely noticed it.

Quinn pulled her down beside him on the bench by the swimming hole. “This is a little piece of heaven.” He took a deep breath, then let it out slowly. Ellie sensed the tension easing from his shoulders.

“Are you behind on the work?” she asked worriedly.

“Nothing I can’t find time for later.” He kissed the top of her head. “I can work anytime now. I’ll save the noisy bits for the daytime and work on the quieter stuff at night.”

They sat quietly for a few minutes, as Cali dashed about the woods as if hunting for game. “I can’t wait to see what you’re hiding under that cloth.”

“Oh, you caught that, did you?” He shifted in his seat, appearing to grow restless, and finally stood.

Ellie followed. “I take it that’s not part of the main project?”

“No.” He twined his fingers with hers again and they continued their walk in comfortable end-of-day silence.

Cali raced past them as they neared the house and sat by Quinn’s car. Quinn ignored the dog, gathered Ellie in his arms, and kissed her soundly. “I feel like a kid, grabbing stolen kisses, not sure where this is going.”

Ellie snaked her arms around his neck. “That’s exactly how I feel! So, we’ll stop worrying and just be.” She stood on her toes and kissed him deeply, his arms crushing her to him, their breathing rapid.

With reluctance, he pulled away and checked his watch again. “I’ll be a bit late tomorrow morning. I want to pack the last pieces in the truck, and make sure the house is locked up tight.” He shifted to step away, then darted in for a last kiss that made her laugh.

After his car disappeared down the driveway, Ellie stood for a minute, hands deep in her pockets, savouring the night. She pulled out the key to the barn and decided to make Quinn's stay a bit more enjoyable.

For the next hour she gathered items from the house, blankets, pillows, and towels, and made the bedroom stall a cozy destination for Quinn. She latched the upper bunk up and away so he wouldn't bang his head, took out the old double mattress from the storage area and made the lower bed, fluffing the pillows and setting an extra blanket on the end. The bathroom was clean, with new soap in the container and a fresh towel on the hanger.

She surveyed the bedroom stall and made one last trip into the house, gathering a small bedside lamp and the curtains from her daughter's old room to hang over the window above the bed.

She took a step back, satisfied with how she had redone the area. He would sleep well here.

Chapter Seventeen

The storm had rumbled through during the night, leaving a coolness to the air that Ellie appreciated as she and Cali returned from their walk. She was excited about Quinn arriving later in the morning and settling into the barn. Her sleep had been restless, but she still felt invigorated.

Ruth was puttering around the kitchen, making a pot of coffee when Ellie entered. Ellie fed Cali, then joined Ruth at the counter.

"I love the in between rain time," Ruth said, gazing out the window at the sun-backed sparkles from the last droplets hanging on the branches.

"The weatherman is calling for a few more showers this morning, but nothing much."

"They're never right, but the garden certainly needs it."

"And how are you today, Ruth?" Ellie took out a bowl and pancake mix. "How does pancakes sound for breakfast?"

"I'd love that," Ruth answered, a bit of sparkle in her voice. "And I'm doing well, thank you. Slept better than expected. Ellie, who's that?"

A small blue car drove up the driveway and parked near the porch. No one got out. Cali sat at the door, her tail thumping and her butt shaking from side to side.

It surprised Ellie to see her Aunt Norma exit the car and climb the steps of the porch.

"Good morning to you," Norma smiled, letting herself in.

"Aunt Norma!" Ellie moved in for a hug. Her Aunt Norma was the eclectic part of the family. Her father's older sister, widowed for several years, but still full of life and style. Today she wore a Yoda t-shirt under a plaid sweater, red jeans and green tennis shoes. And somehow it all came together like a fashion magazine spread.

"What brings you by so early in the morning?" Ellie asked, ushering her into the kitchen.

"Breakfast, Norma?" Ruth asked. "We're having pancakes."

"Gosh, no, thanks." Norma sank onto a chair. "I just dropped by to ask you why you're selling? Where are you and Shirley moving to?"

Ruth and Ellie both froze, not sure if they had heard right.

"I have no idea what you're talking about." Ruth braced a hand against the counter. "I'm not moving anywhere."

"Well," Norma leaned on the table, hands clasped, frowning in confusion. "There's a For Sale by Owner sign on your front lawn, and a young couple was walking in when I drove by."

"What were you doing at the Tiny House Haven at this time of the morning?" Ellie asked.

"Tess and I had breakfast." Norma shifted in her seat. Everyone was aware of how Norma avoided most people due to her dislike of small talk. But she and Tess had become fast friends over the years, easing into it over their mutual love of science fiction movies. "She's trying to get me to join your genealogy group."

"That would be..." Ellie started.

Ruth grabbed her sweater from the back of her chair and headed out the door. Breakfast was forgotten.

"Wait, Ruth!" Ellie called. "Where are you going?"

"She's not selling my home from under me," Ruth growled. Anger sparked from her eyes.

"Hold on," Ellie snatched her keys and nodded for Norma to follow them. "Let's take a minute and calm down. We'll go together and check it out. Maybe it's a mistake."

"Nope," Norma said. "There's a sign, and Shirley has an early morning viewing going on as we speak."

Ruth marched out and waited at the car for Ellie to lock up and join her. Norma climbed in the back, Ruth in the front, and they were off.

***

No one spoke on the short drive over, but Ruth's hand kept a steady tapping on the armrest.

They arrived to find a sign was indeed on Ruth's front lawn advertising For Sale by Owner, and there was a strange car in the driveway. Through the screen door, they heard a conversation coming from the living room.

Ruth scrambled out of her seat, not waiting for anyone, and made it up the two steps and onto the porch in record time.

"Ruth, wait!" Ellie caught her by the arm and steadied her. "Don't go in all angry. Calm yourself first."

Norma was behind them, ready to lend a hand. "I can't believe this," she muttered. Ellie sent her a warning glare. Norma shrugged, as if she had no clue how to proceed.

Ruth took a few deep breaths, gave Ellie a nod, then flung the door wide. They followed her inside.

"Shirley!" Ruth called. "What's going on?"

The conversation in the other room ceased. Shirley came into the hall, a young couple right on her heels, their eyes wide with surprise. The tension in the closed confines raised the hairs on Ellie's arm.

Shirley recovered her shock at seeing her sister, and lifted her head as if going into battle. "Since you're moving on with your life, I will too. So, first things first, we'll sell the house."

"I never gave you permission to do this," Ruth sputtered.

Ellie put a gentle hand on Ruth's arm. "Maybe we should talk about this."

"There's nothing to talk about," Shirley blustered. "You're leaving me to find this man, and I will be on my own."

"Not that again!" Ruth shook her head as if Shirley's words were pure nonsense.

The young couple edged along the wall towards the exit and out. "We'll discuss this between us and get back to you," the man said to Shirley through the door.

"But you haven't seen the bedrooms yet," Shirley said frantically, racing to the porch after them.

"There's nothing to discuss," Ruth said as they all moved outside. "The house is not for sale."

The couple's car pulled out quickly and disappeared down the road.

"What do you think you're doing?" Ruth yelled at her sister.

Ellie and Norma had stepped off the porch, giving them room. Now everyone stood stock still in shock. No one had ever heard Ruth raise her voice. The whites of her eyes were showing, and her hand shook as she pointed at her sister.

A few neighbors had stepped out on their stoops to see what the commotion was about. Ruth normally hated being the centre of drama, but at this moment she paid them no mind.

"If you're going to leave and live with your boyfriend, I can't stay here by myself. We'll split the sale price and go our own ways." Shirley stood her ground but her forehead was bathed in sweat.

"Did you think you could do this and I'd never find out?" Ruth stormed down the stairs as best as a 92-year-old could, and tugged at the For Sale sign, trying to dislodge it. Her frustration at not being able to move it even an inch had Ellie running forward to take over. It wasn't buried deep, and Ellie managed to yank it out after a few solid tugs.

Ruth grabbed it from her and threw it in the back of the car. "My home is not for sale!"

"Ruth, stop, please." Ellie forced the older woman to focus on her. "Calm down. This is not good for your heart."

But Shirley was bracing herself for a fight. "I can indeed sell this house if I want to." Her bravado carried to the few neighbours gawking at them. The two sisters fighting on their front lawn was something no one had ever imagined would happen.

"You have no right," Ruth said slowly. "This house is in my name. It is mine."

"And you let me live here by your good graces, my Lady?" Shirley sneered at her sister, though her eyes held fear, not anger.

"Shirley," Ellie said. "This is not the time for this."

Ruth lowered her voice, finally aware of the growing crowd around them. "I'm not moving anywhere. I will be back when I'm back. We will talk when I'm ready, and you will live with that." She shook so hard her teeth chattered.

Norma stepped forward and took her arm. "Let's get you back to Ellie's. A cup of tea would do us all a world of good." She guided Ruth back to the car.

Ellie felt at a loss. "She's not leaving you, Shirley."

Shirley hadn't moved, as if frozen by shame on her own front lawn.

Ruth struggled into the car and slammed the door. Slamming of doors appeared to give her pleasure. But it made Ellie wince.

Ellie studied Shirley. She appeared to be hanging on to her dignity by a slim thread. "Shirley," Ellie started, but the older turned sharply and disappeared inside, banging the door tight behind her. Everyone heard the lock slide closed with a thud.

Ellie stared at the few straggling neighbors. "The show's over folks. Hope you enjoyed it." They had the grace to drop their eyes and leave.

Norma climbed into the back seat, moving the For Sale sign over so she could squeeze her legs in and sit. Ruth was once again tapping her fingers on the armrest, eager to go, her shaking subsiding.

Ellie's walk to the car was slower. Her emotions were in a turmoil over what had just happened between the sisters. She eased behind the wheel and they headed back to her place, each lost in their own thoughts.

An invisible cloud hovered over what had been a promising new day.

Chapter Eighteen

The three women piled into Ellie's home just as the rain started. Removing sweaters, laying purses on the hall table, shuffling out of outdoor shoes. It was a quiet routine.

"I'm still making pancakes, Ruth, and you're going to eat them," Ellie declared as she took out some bowls and a frying pan.

"Oh, no I'm not," Ruth started, but hesitated at Ellie's piercing look.

"You need to eat."

"But we don't need to talk," Norma piped in, "at least not if you don't want to."

Ruth sat down and shook her head. "I can't believe she did that."

"Did what?" Quinn asked, having caught her comment as he walked through the front door. "What did I miss?"

Ellie gave him a tight smile and a quick nod in Ruth's direction before focusing on her pancakes. Batter ready and pan hot, she dropped dollops onto the hot surface. While they were cooking, she set the kettle to boil for tea.

Ruth faced him and squared her shoulders. "My sister tried to sell our home without consulting me."

Quinn strolled over to the table and settled into a seat across from Ruth. He nodded at Norma, who held out a hand. "I'm Norma, Ellie's aunt on her father's side."

"Nice to meet you," he shook her tiny hand. "I'm Quinn, renter of the barn. Love the t-shirt."

"Thank you." Norma's surprise was evident, but Ellie mouthed "later" to her for a detailed explanation of why Quinn was in her house.

He took Ruth's hand in his. "So, tell me what happened."

Ruth let him hold her hand, and leaned forward as if about to share a secret. "My father left this home to me in his will. Shirley has never been good with money, or paying bills, or that such."

"But she runs her own landscaping business," Norma pointed out.

"She does," Ruth acknowledged. "But that was only after my father died, many years after. And when we sold this house to Ellie and Adam, the proceeds came to me. And with those proceeds, I bought the smaller home in the Tiny House Haven."

"It's not really a tiny house, though," Norma said.

Ellie gave her a warning shake of the head, so Norma shrugged and sat back to listen to the story. Ellie brought a cup of tea to Ruth, and Ruth wrapped her hands around the warm mug. Another was passed to Norma and Quinn shook his head no, to, Ellie's tilt of the head question.

"So why was she trying to sell your home?" Quinn asked.

"Because she's sure I'm leaving her." Ruth started to cough.

Ellie's eyes flew to her as Ruth shivered. Before she spoke another word, Ellie had draped Ruth's sweater around her shoulders, then dashed back to the stove and flipped over the pancakes.

"Why would you leave her?" Quinn seemed confused.

"She thinks I'm setting out to find Jeremy, and if I find him, that I'll leave her behind and go off with him."

"What rubbish!" Norma snorted.

Ruth coughed again, her hand covering her mouth. Ellie stepped over and checked Ruth's forehead, roles now reversed. "You're warm."

"I'm okay." Ruth took a sip of her tea and managed a weary smile. "This whole mess has caught up to me, is all."

Ellie waited beside her, unsure what to do.

Ruth glanced over at the stove. "I bet those would taste wonderful if they don't burn."

Ellie turned to see light tendrils of smoke rising from the pan. "Oh, jeesh!" Ellie raced to pull the pan off the heat, flipping the pancakes over to reveal only one had a small portion of it's edge darkened. "Saved!" She brought a plate to Ruth, putting the butter and maple syrup alongside it. "Please eat this, Ruth. Even just little bites to start."

"She had a for sale sign on the front lawn and was showing a young couple the house when we got there!" Ruth said, taking the knife and fork Quinn handed to her before cutting a small piece.

"Ruth," Ellie said. "Were you aware Shirley has a medical condition?"

Ruth stopped chewing and grimaced. "You mean her bossyitis?"

"That's not an actual condition," Norma laughed.

"You'd be surprised." Ruth took another bite.

"Dr. Eastman asked me to keep an eye on her," Ellie said, as she sank into a seat beside Quinn.

Ruth hesitated. "No, she never told me. She always flaunted that she had a clean bill of health, and I was the one taking pills."

"Well, talk to her, because she's not telling the truth."

"Does she ever?" Ruth asked, letting out a small sigh, as if even the motions of lifting her knife and fork were taxing.

"Do you need to see the doctor?" Ellie asked.

Between bites of pancake, Ruth said, "Not at all. I spent too much time thinking last night and not enough sleeping. And then with this morning's activities, I probably need a day of... what do you call it — chilling?" She was quiet for a moment. "I don't want anything bad to happen to Shirley, and I'm not moving or selling. But Lord knows that woman can be a trial sometimes."

"You're a wonderful sister, Ruth," Quinn said. "We're all living our own lives at the same time, and sometimes we get our wires crossed, or we get scared or thoughtless."

"Or all the above," Norma said.

"Well, I'll give this all a lot of consideration, but I'm not going back yet."

"Nor do you have to," Ellie assured her. Since Norma and Quinn had declined her offer, Ellie served herself a couple of pancakes from the plate on the table. "I've a meeting with a client this morning, but Quinn will be around."

"I don't need a babysitter." Ruth took her second pancake from Ellie's plate, and Ellie sighed with relief for comfort food that Ruth enjoyed.

"Well, I'm going to settle my things in the barn, and I'll be back." Quinn left quickly, not waiting to hear Ruth's comments about how she was old enough to look after herself.

"And I need to go shopping," Norma said, giving Ruth a quick hug before adjusting her sweater with a slight tug. "I'll see you at the next genealogy meeting, Ruth. You'll get through this. Don't forget, there are many people around you to help." She gave a firm nod and left them with their mouths gaping.

"Did Norma just hug me?" Ruth asked.

"She's full of surprises these days," Ellie said. "And as far as Quinn goes, he'll be working most of the day, but he'll be within earshot. And Cali will be here."

Hearing her name, the dog appeared at Ruth's side like magic. Cali had a sense of when people needed her most, and had latched on to Ruth from the moment she'd walked into the room. Cali also knew better than to approach people when they were eating, so she stretched out at Ruth's feet under the table and waited.

Ruth finished buttering her pancake and lowered her knife, giving Ellie her full attention. "Perhaps I don't want to know what happened to Jeremy. Shirley told him I didn't wait and had gone off and married someone else. Why in the world would he want anything to do with me now?"

Ellie squeezed Ruth's hand. "We'll do whatever you want, whenever you want."

"But what if he *is* still alive and if I wait too long and he passes?" Her eyes glistened.

They sat in silence, each considering the implications of waiting, and the possibility of a negative reaction to them finding Jeremy. "Ruth," Ellie murmured. "I'm not telling you what to do, but if you don't find him, you'll never know for sure. You can tell him what happened. One way or the other, don't you want to find out?"

Ruth bowed her head, hands in her lap, fingers massaging her aching joints. "I do, but I'm afraid."

"How about I cancel my appointment this morning and we..."

Ruth's head snapped up. "Absolutely not! You'll not change your life anymore than you already have for me. I'm a grown woman and I can make these decisions and not crumple."

"That's the truth." Ellie admired her friend as Ruth gathered her invisible armour around herself. Ruth was obviously exhausted, both physically and mentally, but she was strong.

Quinn walked in just as Ellie checked the clock on the wall.

"Off you go," Ruth told her. To Quinn, she said, "She's hovering."

"Off you go," Quinn parroted Ruth and gave Ellie a quick hug. "We'll be fine. I want to wait till the rain eases before moving the stuff inside. So..." he looked around the kitchen, "... I'm going to make Ruth some chicken soup."

"Oh, goodness, no," Ruth said. "I'm fine, and I don't want to take up your time."

"No one takes up my time unless I let them." Quinn searched the cupboards, pulling ingredients out, then plunked a pot on the stove. "You still here?" he asked Ellie, who was now standing at the front door, files in hand, eyes wide in surprise at him in her kitchen. "I *can* cook, you know."

"Right, well." Ellie shrugged to Ruth, and Ruth smiled at her and motioned her on her way. Ellie was thankful for the spark of interest in Ruth's eyes. "See you later then."

The door closed behind her.

***

Quinn grinned at Ruth. "I thought she'd never leave. Now we can talk."

Quinn set out the last ingredients for his soup on the island, and wondered what it was about this little woman that brought out his protective instincts. He glanced over at Ruth as she fiddled with her cup, her gaze riveted out the window to the forest beyond, eyes lost in a far-off memory.

He dove in with the question he was most curious about. "Ruth, did you ever search for Jeremy over the years?"

She dragged her gaze back and frowned at him. "No. When I thought he had never answered my letters, or come for me after the war, I was devastated. Shirley told me I should be glad to be rid of a rotten apple before our relationship had gone further."

"Oh, Ruth." He stopped chopping a carrot. "I'm sorry you had to go through that."

Ruth shuddered at the memory. "I needed her excuses to be true. It felt easier somehow to believe he'd lost interest. But deep down in my heart, I knew Shirley was wrong."

"So, what did you do?"

"I got a teaching degree, and all those children through the years, they became my family. I wouldn't change that part of my life at all, because I loved it." They were quiet for a few minutes before Ruth surprised him with a question of her own. "And why is there no Mrs. Walsh in your life?"

Quinn froze in mid-chop and slowly angled his head so his scar was in full view. "I scare the ladies away."

"Ellie doesn't seem scared."

"She's different."

"She is that, and I don't want her hurt."

Quinn felt her eyes boring into him.

"What are your intentions?"

"Well, *Mom*..." he tried to lighten the mood.

“I’m not joking—not about Ellie,” Ruth said. “She’s been through a lot. Losing her parents at twelve, then Adam and that darling Winnie, it nearly destroyed her. You’re the first man she’s shown any interest in, in years. I was getting worried.”

Quinn’s chest seemed to rise at her words.

“Calm down, cock of the walk,” she cautioned, getting to her feet and taking her cup to the sink. “You’ll have to earn her.”

“I’m aware of that, and I’m terrified of doing or saying the wrong thing.”

Ruth studied him for a moment. “The secret is just be you, and let her be her. If you’re in a rush, you’re doomed. That girl is slow as molasses.”

"I'm patient." He scooped his chopped vegetables into the stock in the pot. He quickly sliced the cooked chicken breasts from the fridge and added them, before covering the pot and lowering the heat.

“I’m going to watch a show,” Ruth said as she settled in on the couch and pulled the blanket over her legs. The washing up sounds from the kitchen became soothing background noises.

***

“The rain stopped, so I’m off,” Quinn declared cheerfully a short while later. “We’ll let this simmer for a couple of hours and it’ll be ready for lunch.” He wiped his hands, ready to go, but stopped short at hearing Ruth gasp. He followed her gaze; Shirley stood in the doorway.

“Not now,” Ruth whispered.

Shirley had stepped inside and let the door slam behind her.

“Not now, Shirley,” Quinn repeated Ruth’s words, but loud enough for her sister to hear them.

“I’d like to speak to my sister!”

Quinn could see she was ready for a fight.

She advanced into the room, her chin jutting. “We need to talk.”

Ruth neither budged nor looked her way. She grabbed the remote control and clicked on the TV, found Wynonna Earp and drowned out her sister’s voice with the comforting twang of Doc Holliday’s words.

"Come home, now, Ruth!" Shirley took another aggressive step forward, but Quinn stopped her. "I think I'm getting sick," she called past him into the living room." And I'm not eating well, and I – I can't sleep because that noise in the fridge needs to be adjusted and you're the only one who can do it." The words tumbled out, one behind the other without a break for a breath. And then she waited, as if her plight would compel Ruth to return home with her. Shirley didn't apologize for putting the house up for sale or causing a scene hours earlier. It was as if it had never happened.

Ruth ignored her, her frozen stature and controlled deep breaths telling Quinn she was hanging on as best she could.

"Shirley," he said, "I'll take you home and give you some of this chicken soup for supper." He moved quickly into the kitchen and scooped some soup into a container, keeping a sharp eye on her in case she tried to head into the living room. He slapped a cover on the container and went to Shirley. "Let's go."

He ushered her out, wondering how he could feel sorry for someone who had ruined her sister's hopes and dreams in such a heartless manner. "Back soon, Ruth," he called over his shoulder before firmly closing the door, taking Shirley's car keys from her unresisting hands and hustling her into the passenger seat. A quick walk back through the woods would do him good.

"I can drive, you know," she muttered, but didn't offer any resistance. She sank into her seat as if all the fight had left her.

It took minutes to get to Ruth and Shirley's house in the Tiny House Haven community. Quinn followed Shirley inside. "What's this fridge noise you were talking about?"

"It's fine." Shirley seemed ashamed to be caught in another lie. "I just need Ruth to come home."

"Shirley." Quinn put the soup on the counter. "She needs some TLC right now."

"So do I!" Shirley wailed. It made Quinn's ears hurt to hear the self-pity in her voice until he looked at her closely. Her hair was unbrushed, her sweater buttoned wrong, and her eyes were red rimmed, as if from crying.

He kept his tone calm. "I'm sure she'll be home soon. But maybe you should think about what you're going to say to her to make this better, if that can happen."

"What *I* can say?" Shirley said, as if the thought of it being her responsibility to make amends with Ruth had never occurred to her. But he saw it in the way her eyes shifted from side to side, as if looking for the least painful exit. None of this would be painless, for either sister.

"Right." He dismissed her comment. "The soup needs to be on the stove for a couple of hours to finish cooking at a low temperature, then you're ready." He headed for the door then stopped. "And Shirley, let Ruth come home on her own terms. Don't keep pressuring her. The doctor says she needs to rest."

"As if I'd do anything to hurt...," Shirley blustered then stopped, maybe hearing her own words for the first time. "Fine," she said in a huff, then disappeared down the hall to the kitchen where he could hear a pot banging onto the stove.

Chapter Nineteen

When Ellie walked in from her client appointment, she found Ruth stretched out on the couch, dozing in and out, Wynonna Earp playing on the tv. The squeak of the closing front door caused Ruth to sit up in surprise. She pushed her hair back into place with one hand, and adjusted the surrounding blankets with the other.

"I'm sorry, Ellie," she fussed a bit more with her sweater and fumbled for the remote at the same time. "I did not expect to be sleeping the day away."

Ellie felt Ruth's forehead. "No fever, but after what you've just been through, you deserve a little laze-about time." She sat on the couch beside Ruth, put her computer on the coffee table, and dropped her files on the floor at her feet.

"Rough meeting?" Ruth asked, freezing the episode of the show for later.

"She wants a lot of information about her family history, but doesn't have much to start with." Ellie stretched her arms above her head and let her body sink into the cushions. "But you know me, I *do* so love a mystery. Don't stop watching your show, Ruth." She leaned her head back and settled in as if the show held her attention. But Ruth flicked the TV off.

"Have you planned out the lesson you'll be giving to the class on Thursday?" Ruth asked.

Ellie fidgeted in her seat, not answering. When Ruth gave Ellie her famous teacher stare, Ellie finally blurted out. "Not at all! I hate public speaking! I've only ever taught the seniors, and I..." She cleared her throat and blinked her eyes to stop the wetness forming.

Ruth shifted in her seat until her shoulder was touching Ellie's. "I know they were Winnie's friends and seeing them again will bring it all back, but have you ever thought that maybe they *want* to see you? A lot of them spent days here, swimming in the pond, sleeping in the barn, running around the woods like banshees. I'm sure they miss that, and they miss you. You were the *cool* mom."

Ellie turned to her in disbelief. "How in the world would you know that?"

"People talk." Ruth shrugged a shoulder as if it was common knowledge. "I taught most of their parents over the years, and they're all so proud of their own children. And rightly so. And they talk. Losing a child is every parent's worst nightmare. No one knew how to help you then, but they all like you, Ellie."

Ellie shifted again in her seat.

"I've always found that it's good to start with a small idea, and let things grow from that," Ruth suggested.

Ellie grabbed her notebook from the side-table. "Actually, I've got a few ideas, like things I'd liked to have known about my own parents." She flipped through the pages, removed the pen from the metal spiral, and clicked it open when she arrived at the notes.

"And what would that be?" Ruth quirked an eyebrow at her.

Ellie tapped the pen on the page and frowned. "Well, I've heard the stories about how they met, but from other people. I wish I had their version, their inner thoughts, what they thought of each other."

"Your mother didn't like your father right away," Ruth answered. Ellie raised an eyebrow in disbelief. "Oh, there was nothing wrong with him—he was so earnest, so serious about life."

"What? Dad was the funniest man I knew. Being serious was the *last* thing Dad was, unless it had to do with our safety."

"Your mom had a great sense of humour." Ruth said. "She loved practical jokes, and some of them fell pretty flat, but he never held them against her. You know that trick where you put water in a bucket on the top of a half-opened door and..."

"She didn't!" Ellie laughed. "I can't believe that."

"Oh, she did, and it was at school."

"Did she get in trouble?"

Ruth let out a small laugh. "She had it timed and planned for your dad to walk through, but it was the principal, Mr. Eason, who walked in and got soaked."

Ellie shook her head in wonder as she pictured her mother setting up a practical joke. "I never heard that one."

"It was lucky Mr. Eason was also a football coach, so he had a change of clothes at school. But your mother had to clean up the mess, and was in detention for a week."

"A week is pretty easy."

"Not when it's spring, the weather's lovely, and all your friends were outside having fun. Including your father. He actually sat under a tree outside the class window where your mother spent those five long days of detention. He was a nice man."

Ellie sat back and considered what Ruth had told her. "It's funny how we never see our parents as being people in their own right, having had pasts, good and bad, hopes and dreams. To their children they're just parents."

"No one is ever *just* a parent," Ruth said.

"Then that's what I'll do." Ellie jotted a few quick notes. "This will be a fun class. I'll show them how to find questions they've always wanted to know about, and how to get their parents to answer." She looked over at Ruth, her enthusiasm suddenly slipping away. "Ruth, I don't know if I can stand in front of all those familiar faces, and not see Winnie sitting there with them."

Ruth pulled her tight, wrapping her arms around the younger woman for a deep squeeze before releasing her. "There's no denying the first few minutes will be hard. For all of you. But I think Winnifred would be so proud you're doing this for her friends."

"My legs will shake, and what if I blubber in front of them?"

"Then you take out a tissue, wipe your eyes, and go on with the lesson." Ruth produced a tissue from her sleeve and handed it to Ellie with a flourish. "It's like magic!"

Ellie felt her panic ease a bit, and like the coward she thought she was, quietly asked, "Would you come with me?"

"I think that would be a grand idea. I would love to see the inside of the school again. Did you know if you go behind the woodworking section, teachers can't see you?"

Ellie tried to hide a grin. "Really?"

"Said the woman who spent recess there with the bad boys."

"They thought they were bad. I was just studying them."

Ruth let out a hoot. Her stomach let out a noisy growl. "My goodness, almost lunchtime."

As Ellie moved to get up, Ruth grabbed her by the arm. "Not to worry, Quinn put a lovely chicken soup together for us."

"Why don't you relax for a bit while I go check Cali isn't getting under Quinn's feet."

"Of course, you're *only* going to check on Cali. You're a good dog owner after all."

Ellie adjusted her jean jacket, refusing to take the bait. A quick grin was all she gave Ruth as she left.

***

Cali ran to her as she entered the barn, dashing around her legs like they had been apart for months. Ellie hunkered down and gave her a good head scratch, glancing up to see Quinn hand-sanding a finely turned table leg on his workbench. He was so focused he didn't realize she was there until Cali ran back to him and nudged his leg.

He caught her hovering in the door.

"I'm sorry," she said, "I didn't mean to interrupt, but that delicious soup will be ready for lunch in about," she glanced at her watch, "ten minutes?"

He stretched the muscles in his back. "I'm about done with this."

Ellie walked further into the barn and strolled from one piece to another, some still resting on machines, others, like two other table legs leaning against the workbench. She ran her fingers across the smooth grain of the finished work then moved to the largest item, the dining room table. It could easily seat eight people with the middle leaf, and the sun hit the deep grain of the wood as it rested against the wall, making it shine.

"This is quite the piece." She walked around it. "Do they have a big house?"

"They do. And they've commissioned a bedroom set."

Ellie raised an eyebrow and nodded. "That will be a huge project."

"Shirley came by," Quinn said.

"What?" Ellie was surprised. "She has some nerve. I hope she apologized."

"Not a word. But Ruth refused to speak with her and I drove her home with some soup." He continued working on the bottom of the leg. "Do you think Ruth will be okay?"

She noted the sure and steady strokes his hand made as it pushed the sand paper gently against the lower edge of the leg. It made a gentle scratching noise that seemed to echo in the barn. "I think she'll adjust. When my family died, I thought I'd never recover, and it was Ruth who visited me each day. Sometimes she'd just sit beside me and we'd watch life go by. Sometimes she talked; about everyday things, nothing of consequence, but topics that had me answering her many questions. Even when I didn't want to. Then finally she bullied me into getting back into life, shamed me really."

She caught his eye. He was listening carefully, all attention focused on her. Ellie pushed away from the wall and approached him. "Ruth said life is worth living and we're all entitled to the grieving period, but not to wasting away. I wasn't aware of what she'd gone through herself when she said those words."

Quinn wiped his hands on the rag hanging from his jeans and tossed it on the bench. "She's a wise woman."

Ellie put her arms around Quinn's neck and leaned in. "She is indeed. She puts that little nugget of information in your head and lets it grow."

"Is this a nugget?" He reached for her and their bodies eased together.

"This is not letting a good thing slip past." She kissed him gently, leaning into him as he deepened the kiss.

"It would be a shame to let a good thing slip past us," he murmured against her lips, his hands stroking her back, a mix of comfort and promises of more to come. "Life is short and all that." He bent to kiss her again when someone cleared their throat.

Ruth was framed in the doorway; the rain having ended and rays of sun peaking through the tree branches behind her. "I'm starving."

If there had been suction between them, Ellie and Quinn would have separated with a pop. They both talked at once, moving about, filling the space, embarrassed to be caught in each other's arms.

But then Ellie abruptly stopped, angry with herself for feeling as if she had done something wrong. "We were kissing." She put a hand on her hip and struck a "so what" pose.

Ruth raised one eyebrow, and headed back to the house. "Good for you, but I'm still hungry," she called over her shoulder.

Chapter Twenty

Ruth was nowhere to be found when they walked into the kitchen minutes later. Quinn washed his hands while Ellie sliced a baguette and set it out with bowls of Quinn's steaming chicken soup.

Ruth returned, having changed into her usual attire of comfortable pants, white blouse, and pastel sweater. What Ellie had come to refer to as her armor. Ellie was relieved to see some color back in Ruth's face.

The meal passed quickly, the sun outside lifting everyone's mood, and when Quinn added some of his horrible knock-knock jokes, there were good-natured groans all around.

Ellie and Ruth settled in the living room once the meal was done, and Quinn disappeared back to the barn. Ruth folded the blanket and placed it at the end of the couch, as if declaring she wouldn't be needing any coddling, thank you very much.

She picked up the tv selector and turned it in her hand, as if weighing whether she'd disappear into her show again. Ellie opened her laptop and sat back, tapping the mouse back and forth on her knee.

"This elephant in the room is rather big, isn't it?" Ruth said.

"And what elephant would that be?" Ellie pretended ignorance, not wanting to push the subject one way or the other.

"What would you do next to find Jeremy, if I wanted to?" Ruth picked an invisible piece of lint from her pants.

Ellie sat forward and started the computer. "Well, I think one of the easiest things would be to check out Facebook, see if he has a presence there."

"My goodness, Facebook!" Ruth blinked nervously.

"Do you want me to look?"

Ruth sat for a minute, and Ellie could see the countless emotions warring within her, as if she were weighing the pros and cons of taking this momentous step forward.

"Yes." Ruth clasped her hands together. "Yes, I think that's what we should do. Will he know what we're doing?" Her eyes widened at the thought.

Ellie smiled at her. "No, he won't know." She loaded her Facebook account and entered Jeremy's name in the search box. Ruth raised her hand as if to say "stop", and then lowered it, motioning instead for her to continue. Ellie put a book under the machine on her lap and angled it so Ruth could see.

"There are three Jeremy Butlers listed here, but the pictures appear to be too young to be him."

Ruth squinted at the screen and shook her head. "No." The word came out slowly and drawn out. "I don't think so."

"Let me put in the last name," Ellie typed it in. Numerous responses appeared, and they both sat back.

"There's too many," Ruth said. "How can we narrow this down?"

"Do you know what Jeremy's father's name was? If he had a son, maybe he named him after his dad."

"Try Sam Butler."

Ellie typed it in, and two entries came up. Ruth glanced at the first one and gasped. "Oh, my, that's him!"

Ellie saw a younger man, perhaps in his sixties, though he bore a striking resemblance to the drawing Ruth had made of Jeremy. "Let's see." She hit the button and opened the man's page; surprised and grateful he hadn't put strict privacy restrictions on it. She scrolled slowly until Ruth waved at her to stop.

"There," Ruth whispered. She pointed at a picture in the photo section of the man and an older gentleman playing chess. The older man's hand was raised in victory.

Ellie clicked on the photo and attached to it was the caption "Dad and I playing chess. He beat me again." Beside the photo was an identification tag that read "Sam Butler is with Jeremy Butler."

"Oh, my," Ruth cried, as she stared at the face of her beloved Jeremy.

"Are you sure?"

"He loved chess, and I hated it!" Ruth laughed. "My dad used to play with him, and Jeremy always won. He was so smart."

Ellie scrolled down further, but there was nothing more of interest. "Shall we get in touch with Sam, see if he can connect us with Jeremy?"

Ruth couldn't tear herself away from the picture, then she noted the date. "That was two years ago, Ellie. Perhaps he's..."

"Well," Ellie wouldn't let her finish. "Even if he is, we'll find out what happened. I'll leave Sam a message to call me."

"You won't mention me though?" Ruth was aghast at the possibility.

"Of course not," Ellie soothed her. "I'll say that I have some information to share about his father before the war. Something like that." She typed out a message quickly, but hesitated before sending. "Ruth, do you want to hit send?"

Ruth's eyes sparkled with excitement, anticipation, and hope. "Yes." She leaned over and hit the send button.

"And now we wait." Ellie leaned back.

"I hate waiting," Ruth grumbled.

"Then let's go for a walk," Ellie suggested, turning off her computer and reaching out to Ruth. Ruth accepted the helping hand, and they headed out into the sunny afternoon, Cali alongside them as Ellie grabbed the dog's throw toy off the porch.

***

By the end of the day, the ladies were frazzled. They had been sure this was their Jeremy's son, but as the day wore on, doubts clouded their excitement. They filled the afternoon and evening with checking Ellie's phone for messages, minor chores, walking Cali more than usual, checking Ellie's phone, cooking supper, cleaning up, settling in for mindless television watching, and, of course, checking Ellie's phone yet again.

Nothing.

By nine o'clock exhaustion had taken Ruth to bed. Ellie's optimism and enthusiasm had dwindled during the day and by the time the older woman left the room, shoulders drooping and her steps slow, Ellie worried she had made a mistake getting their hopes up at all.

But not normally being a negative Nelly, she grabbed a light jacket and headed out to the barn to tell Quinn it was last walk. She could get used to having him around at meals, and hearing the creative sawing and hammering coming from the barn. Ellie passed the hall mirror and caught sight of the smile that felt plastered on her face for the last couple of days whenever she thought of him. She was starting a relationship with Quinn, and the usual acid response in her stomach at such a thought had never materialized. She gave herself a thumbs up and headed out to get Cali from her new favourite spot, anywhere near Quinn. Lucky dog.

She found Quinn slouched on a chair, arms crossed, expression grim as he stared at one of the table legs, broken and in pieces on the bench in front of him.

Ellie looked from him to the table leg and raised an eyebrow, waiting for an explanation.

He picked up the piece. "Sometimes trying to do that one bit extra is a disaster." He showed her a deep cut where the break had occurred. "I was adding a delicate–well, never mind, it didn't work." He tossed it onto the ground and took a deep breath.

"What does this mean for the project?"

He looked at her, stretched his arms overhead and swivelled to get the ever-present crick out of his back. "Another day of work, which is not in the schedule, but I *am* getting this delivered on time." He motioned her to a pile of wood at the side of the barn and searched through the pieces before pulling out a length and showing it to her. He measured it against the three completed legs. "I almost didn't get an extra piece of this."

"Gut instinct?" Ellie asked, reaching over to stroke Cali, who sat nearby, waiting patiently for their walk.

"More like a voice in my head." He looked out at the darkness falling through the barn door. "Last call?"

"I'll take her alone so you can keep working."

"No." He dusted his hands off on his jeans and reached out to her. "I've been waiting for this all day."

Fingers clasped, they headed down the forest path in silence. The day had not warmed as expected, and the cool breeze was gentle against their faces. Cali took off, always bringing her toy back for Quinn to throw.

They strolled slowly, taking their customary seats on the bench at the pond, watching the last of the sun's rays disappearing behind the trees and the stars glistening in the sky. Quinn leaned against the rock wall and let out a sigh. He kept her hand tight in his, and she leaned into him, enjoying his warmth.

"I hope... you don't think I'm... going really slow here." Quinn stumbled over his words. "It's been a while since I've been with anyone I wanted to be serious with."

Ellie gazed at him in the fading light. "I think the pace is perfect."

"Doesn't mean I don't want to..." he searched for the words, "... have my way with you. It's just that..."

She put a finger to his lips to stop any other thoughts from escaping. "Same with me, but I'd like to get to know you first. Like I don't even know your favourite color!"

"Racing green."

She grinned. “Do you like F1 racing? Racing green always reminds me of it. When I was a kid my friends thought I was nuts, a girl loving car racing.”

He pulled her onto his lap, wrapping his arms around her. She nestled her head into the crook of his neck. “You’re a gal after my own heart! I love it. I used to race motorcycles back home, anything fast really.”

Ellie sat away and cupped his cheek. “Please tell me you don’t do that anymore.”

“These old bones?” He laughed. “I ride a motorcycle, but I wouldn’t dream of racing these days. I don’t believe I’m invincible anymore.”

They sat together as the minutes ticked by, Ellie dozing off in his arms before Cali bounded up to them, soaking wet, and shook the water from her fur.

“Oh, no, Cali!” Ellie hopped up to dodge the droplets but ended with her jeans soaking wet.

Quinn had faired better needing only to wipe his arms before taking Ellie’s hand again. She loved that he didn’t seem to want to break their connection. “Back to work. Sorry about this, but I’ll have to work the next few nights to get this finished on time. Is that okay? I’ll keep the doors shut so there’s not too much noise.”

She squeezed his hand and nodded. “We don't hear anything on the other side of the house, and Ruth sleeps like a rock.”

“And thanks for making it so comfortable for me in the barn.”

“My pleasure. It’s important to have a good place to sleep.”

“And how do *you* sleep?” They had reached the barn, and he pulled her into his arms, one wrapped around her waist and the other cupping the back of her head, waiting for her answer. When she didn’t respond, he leaned down and let his lips graze hers, back and forth, softly. She pressed herself against him, sharing a deep kiss before pulling back and stepping out of his arms.

“I sleep very well, thank you,” she tossed at him before dashing up the stairs and into the house.

“At least one of us will,” he grumbled to himself.

Chapter Twenty-One

Quinn had eaten and resumed work in the barn before Ellie and Ruth wandered into the kitchen at 7:00 a.m. He hadn't made a sound, but had left a pot of oatmeal gently simmering on the stove. Its delicious aroma of cinnamon filled their noses.

"Shall I?" Ellie held up a bowl to Ruth, nodding towards the pot.

"Yes, please," Ruth answered, retrieving milk from the fridge. "Who knew Quinn could cook as well as build furniture."

"Hidden talents," Ellie replied, delivering two bowls of hot oatmeal to the table. She found the coffeepot to be three quarters full and shook her head in delight. "He's left us coffee."

"Definitely a keeper." Ruth took a seat and mixed a full teaspoon of brown sugar on top of her breakfast, then added the milk.

Ellie brought the coffee cups and a bag of raisins, and sat down with a sigh. She fixed her oatmeal to her taste and frowned as Ruth sighed. The woman was eating slowly, chewing methodically, and leaning on the table as if it were supporting her.

"Did you not sleep well, Ruth?"

Ruth tried to smile. "It was okay. But I think I've set myself up for another disappointment."

Ellie checked her phone. Seeing there was no response to her message, she flipped it over on the table. "We need to be patient."

"Need, shmeed," Ruth mumbled under her breath. "I'm not a patient person, Ellie. Oh, I know, everyone thinks I am, but if you only knew how often I've wanted to shake people into giving simple answers, or seeing the light about logical things."

"Will you join me in some gardening this morning?" Ellie asked, knowing that any distraction at this point would help them both.

"I can hold a basket, but I don't see myself doing much bending." Ruth nodded at her, a subtle acknowledgement of what Ellie was trying to do, and how much she appreciated it.

Ellie washed her cereal bowl. "I'd like to weed and pick the cherry tomatoes."

"Already?"

"I started some indoors this spring, as an experiment. I planted a few more plants at the normal time, but these three were a month early. I didn't think they'd take, but they're producing right now and I'll have them all summer long."

"Sounds like fun." Ruth headed to the sink to take care of her own dishes, but Ellie took them from her and washed them.

"I'll meet you outside then," Ellie said. She took a quick look out the window. "The sun is just reaching the garden."

"Go take that young man of yours a cup of coffee while I get dressed," Ruth told her as she headed towards her bedroom. "I'm a slow dresser these days." She winked at Ellie as the younger woman filled a mug with coffee.

Ellie hesitated, trying to remember whether he took it black. Why should that be so important all of a sudden?

***

Cali spoiled Ellie's surprise visit by greeting her at the door with a wagging tail. Ellie stood a moment and admired the quick and efficient cuts Quinn made from a piece of wood with a large saw. The man had skills.

His welcoming smile grew when she approached with the steaming cup. "I'm so hoping that's for me." He put the saw down, and gave her a quick kiss before reaching for the cup.

"And if it wasn't?"

"I'd wrestle you for it." He took a deep gulp, his eyes closing. "Beverage of the gods." He moved back to the workbench. "How's Ruth? Any news about Jeremy?"

Ellie strolled around the barn, hands in her pockets, trying for a nonchalant look, though her senses had spiked with his quick kiss. "Nothing yet. Sadly, it can take a few days to hear back from a cold message. Or, he might not get it, or get it and not want to respond, or any number of reasons."

Quinn was back working on the table leg. "That would be rough for Ruth."

"Yeah." Ellie craned her neck to glimpse what he'd hidden under a cloth on the floor behind him, but couldn't see. She knew it was the surprise, and her curiosity was in full bloom. "I think she's of two minds right now, hoping to find information, but also not wanting to get her hopes up."

The sound of the porch door slamming caught their attention. Ruth made her way slowly down the steps, straw sunhat perched on her white hair, a basket for the picked vegetables hooked into the crook of her arm.

"I'm off to my gardening chores." Ellie kissed Quinn before strolling out the door, leaving a bit of mystery and anticipation behind her.

***

Ruth had made it to the barn door and was looking around with interest as Ellie exited. She nodded good morning to Quinn. "Thank you for the breakfast," she said before following Ellie to the garden."

"You're welcome," he called after her.

Ellie snagged a folding chair off the porch as they passed, and placed it in a shady spot near the tomato plants. Ruth sank into it, closed her eyes for a moment to let the early morning garden smell flow over her, then squinted at the cheeky squirrels enjoying the day.

"Well," Ellie's voice brought her back to the present. "There's a lot more tomatoes than I thought. We'll have a lovely salad for lunch today."

"I used to pop so many of them in my mouth when I was working my Ma's garden, that she used to think the plants weren't doing well at all!"

"You're welcome to munch as many as you want here."

With a little sigh she couldn't contain, Ruth handed her the basket.

Walking slowly along the rows, Ellie started picking. "Care to share the burden?"

Ruth took a minute to answer. "My mind is in a whirl and my body's tired. There was a war going on between them all night. I think the clock read one-fifteen just before I finally fell asleep."

Ellie straightened. "If this is causing you such grief, we can stop right now."

"I have a lot of disturbed nights these days." Ruth shifted in her chair as Cali wandered over to see what excitement she was missing. When she realized it was nothing interesting, she planted herself by Ruth's side and enjoyed the head rubs. "I've put this in motion, so let's see what happens. I need to close this chapter."

Ellie nodded and resumed her collecting, and by nine o'clock the garden was in acceptable shape.

And at five past nine, Ellie's phone rang, on the table in the kitchen.

Ellie took Ruth's arm, and they walked as fast as they could into the house. "I'm so sorry, Ruth, I thought I had my phone in my pocket."

"Not to worry," Ruth huffed.

Ellie sprinted ahead, skidded across the slippery kitchen floor, grabbed her phone from the table, and answered breathlessly, "Hello? I'm here!"

"Is this Ellie McLellan?" a deep male voice asked her.

"Yes." She motioned for Ruth to sit at the table.

"My name's Sam. I'm Jeremy's son."

"Oh, my!" Ellie grinned at Ruth. "Can I put you on speaker, please? There's someone else who would like to talk to you. Ruth Cotter."

There was silence, and then Sam's excited voice boomed from her phone. "Ruth Cotter, as in the love of his life, Ruth Cotter? Dad never stops talking about her!"

"He's alive?" Ruth asked, barely daring to believe it.

"Yes, he is." Sam laughed. "He put himself in a retirement home in Fieldstone about two years ago. He's got a wonky knee, and he's recovering from a cold. Gave us quite a shock, thought we might lose him. Other than that, he's doing fine."

Ruth sat in silence, a hand to her mouth. The fact that Jeremy was still alive was overwhelming. "Did you say he's in the retirement home in Fieldstone?"

"Yes, do you know it?"

"It's down the road from me, literally." Ruth choked out, "I – I didn't know."

"He lived in Montreal for most of his life after the war, but he kept saying he wanted to get back to the country."

"We *are* the country," Ellie piped in, as tears flowed over Ruth's cheeks. "So, Sam, tell us about your dad."

"Ruth? Are you okay?" Sam asked.

Ruth dug into her sleeve for the ever-present tissue to wipe her cheeks. Ellie assured him, "She's okay, just overcome with joy at finding Jeremy after all this time,"

"Hey," Sam said excitedly, "do you want me to find out if they'll allow Dad some visitors? The doctors kept him isolated last week, and he's still a bit frail, but I bet he'd love to see you, Ruth."

"Oh, my yes!" Ruth smiled at the possibility and scrubbed at the tears still coursing down.

"I can't promise anything until I get the doctor's okay, but I'll get back to you tonight."

"You sound as excited as Ruth," Ellie said.

"Honestly?" Sam took a deep breath. "My mom died when I was two, and Dad raised me alone. He's a great dad. But it's only in the past ten years that he spoke about his time in the war and before. Ruth was this mystical woman who always made him smile when he talked about her. I can't wait to meet you!"

"And I you, Sam," Ruth said, shaking her head at the dream coming true.

"So, I'll get back to you this evening after I know for sure," Sam promised before signing off.

Ellie said good-bye and grinned at Ruth. "So." Ellie dashed to the stove, her excitement coursing through her body. "Tea is in order, and cookies, lots of cookies."

A deep sob startled her. Ruth was bent over the table, hands to her face, the tears flowing once again, her shoulders heaving.

"Oh, Ruth!" Ellie wrapped her arms tight around Ruth as she continued to sob.

"What's wrong?" Quinn walked into the house to be met with a concerning scene. "Is Ruth hurt?"

Ruth gave him a blinding smile. "He's alive!"

Quinn seemed confused until he realized what they were talking about. "You found him?"

Ruth nodded enthusiastically. "Jeremy is alive, and he's living in a retirement home in Fieldstone." She looked past Quinn to the person on the porch gazing in. No one had heard her approach.

Shirley stood frozen, lips a thin white line, jaw clenched, her hands in tight fists at her sides.

Chapter Twenty-Two

"Shirley," Ellie said, "come in. We have wonderful news."

Shirley refused to move, raising her voice to be heard through the screen. "So, you've found him. I was right! You'll leave me, sell the house, and I'll be shipped to some retirement home with people I don't know!" Her last words came out breathless and shaky.

"Of course not!" Ruth said.

"If you do this, if you go see this man and leave me, I–I don't know what I'll do," Shirley spat out.

Ruth walked over to her sister, keeping the door closed between them. She leaned in, lowered her voice, and stared her down. "You want to keep even this last thread of happiness from me, Shirley? Are you that mean-spirited you would destroy my chances, again? I'm not leaving you, but I'm imagining how wonderful it would be not to live out this drama with you all the time." Ruth shook as she turned and made her way back to the couch. Quinn settled down beside her, his arm going around her frail shoulders.

Ellie was sure Shirley would keep battling, but was surprised when Shirley grabbed at the railing and made her way slowly down the porch steps. Ellie watched the lights of Shirley's car blaze bright.

"I'm through with her dictating what happens in my life!" Ruth declared.

"It *is* your life," Quinn said. "And I honestly don't know how you're even still talking to her. If it were me, her bags would be packed and thrown out the front door. I don't expect you to forgive or forget, but Ruth, I hope you realize that she needs help."

"She's always been afraid of being alone," Ruth said. "But I never thought it was so bad she would blackmail me like this. Never." They sat quietly together until Ruth gathered her strength. With a heavy sigh she stood up, Quinn right behind her, arms out, expecting her to sway. She didn't.

"Ruth, can I..." Ellie watched Ruth's chin rise and her shoulders straighten. She'd seen that stance before in the classroom when the students were getting out of hand.

"I'm fine." She gave them a wobbly smile and headed to the door. "Come, show me what you're working on, Quinn." The door closed behind her and she was halfway down the stairs before Ellie and Quinn snapped out of their surprise.

Quinn raised a questioning eyebrow at Ellie, and she made an "after you" motion. They followed Ruth out of the house to the barn.

***

The day passed in a blur, each of them quiet and contemplative until supper was over and the dishes were once again drying in the rack.

"Are we going to the Cozy tonight?" Ruth asked.

Ellie dried her hands on a towel and leaned back against the counter. "I am, but I wasn't sure if you wanted to."

Ruth pushed in her chair and nodded. "Of course I do. I want them to know what's happened, how their ideas moved things along." Ruth shrugged her shoulders. "Especially tell Phil how his Facebook idea worked. And your ethics topic is a pertinent one."

"And how making floor plans of where you lived can jog your memory." Ellie took a deep breath. Ruth's need to be with her friends was obvious. "Lots to cover tonight. Off we go."

"Wait!" Ruth stopped short. "What if Sam calls back while we're gone?"

Ellie held up her phone. "I'll keep it by my side."

"Fine, fine," Ruth said to herself as she headed to her room to get her purse.

"And I'll get my noisy work done while you ladies are busy elsewhere," Quinn added, giving Ellie a hug and a quick kiss before burying his nose in her hair, taking a deep sniff of her herbal shampoo. "Have I told you I could get used to this?"

"Sniffing my hair?"

"Get a room, you two," Ruth joked as she walked back in.

"I…" Quinn started as Ellie's phone rang. Everyone froze. It rang again.

"Answer it, answer it." Ruth rushed forward, grabbing her arm.

Ellie pulled the phone out of her pocket and opened it. "Hello?" She listened for a moment and then put the phone on speaker for all to hear.

"… and the doctors say he's okay for a brief visit in the morning," said Sam. "How does ten thirty sound?"

"Oh, my!" Ruth's hands shot to her mouth, as if to hold in any whoops of joy from escaping.

"Ruth?" Sam asked. "Is that okay for you?"

"Oh, yes." Ruth's eyes glistened. She blinked rapidly and answered in a rush, "Yes, indeed! I'll be there right on time, and I won't stay long, and I promise not to get him too tired."

Ellie and Quinn both smiled at the joy on the older woman's face. Quinn hugged her, her elation surrounding all of them.

"I'm sure you won't," Sam laughed. "I'll let him know you're coming, and I'll meet you there. Have a good night."

"Oh, dear boy," Ruth said, "this will be the most wonderful night ever."

Ellie hung up and reached for Ruth, gathering her from Quinn and holding her tight until Ruth pulled back slightly. "What are we waiting for? I can't wait to tell everyone I found him!"

She grabbed her purse and was out the door and at the car before Ellie had gathered her own things. "I love it when life works out! Cali's all yours," she called to Quinn as she ran out.

Chapter Twenty-Three

Ruth was out of the car and at the door of the Cozy Corner Café before Ellie had even undone her seatbelt. She gazed at the older woman in wonder at her renewed energy and sparkle. Ruth stopped, motioning enthusiastically for Ellie to hurry.

They walked into the café, arm-in-arm, buddies with a wonderful secret and goofy smiles. Ellie felt the warmth and excitement oozing from Ruth as they caught sight of the rest of the Seniors Genealogy Group waiting for them in the back room.

And Shirley.

Shirley sitting off to one side of the gang, arms folded tightly on the table, eyes boring a hole into her sister as she approached.

"Ellie," Maggie called to her from behind the pastry counter. She waved an envelope at her. "You've got to see this. I need your help."

Ellie looked from the group, now all greeting Ruth and engaging in small talk, and then at her best friend who was bouncing on the balls of her feet. So much energy in this building. Maggie thrust an envelope at her. "Read this."

"What is it?" she asked, taking the letter from the envelope.

Maggie nodded with excitement. "Just read it. It's all there."

Ellie scanned the letter. "Cool, you're getting an inheritance."

"Oh, no," Maggie protested, grinning, "it's much more than that. Can you go through this with me later?"

"Of course." Ellie handed the letter back to her. "How about tomorrow?"

"Uh, no." Maggie blushed. Ellie frowned at her in confusion. Maggie never blushed; she claimed it clashed with her red hair. "I've got plans, but can I make an appointment? I'll need your services."

"Of course, but you've got plans and you're not sharing?" Ellie goaded her. This was getting interesting.

"I'm meeting Pete's parents." Maggie dropped her eyes and muttered as if this declaration would change the world. "He wants me to meet his family." Pete was in the back, helping put together the refreshment tray for the group, but he looked up and gave Ellie a wave, which she returned.

"You are going to *love* Aunt Hannah and Uncle Bill!" Ellie darted in for a quick comforting hug. "And *they're* going to love *you*. Call me when you can." She headed towards the back room only to stop short as the front door banged open.

Ellie spun around to see Norma come barrelling through, wincing at the noise she had made, and gently closing the door behind her. "Sorry," she said to Maggie before giving Ellie a quick hug. "Tess made such a to-do about this group, that I'm very excited to meet everyone." She glanced to the back and took in the members at the table, stopping her sweep when she came to Phil. She gave Ellie a nudge. "Who is that gorgeous man with the lion's head of grey hair?"

Ellie followed her gaze and smiled. "That's Phil. He's rather shy, but a lovely man." She took her aunt's arm and led her back to the group. "Everyone," she called out, "this is my Aunt Norma, and she's going to join us."

Everyone nodded and called out hellos, and Tess waved at her to take a seat between her and Phil. Norma gave Phil a warm smile as he took in her outfit. Red jeans, red running shoes, Star Wars t-shirt, and the much-loved plaid shirt. "Nice shirt," he muttered to her.

"Thank you," she gave him a brilliant smile.

"Continue, Ruth," Doreen said. "You were saying?"

"I was saying the story was actually a real one." Ruth took a deep breath before continuing. "The story was about me, and I found him!" The delight from her was so contagious that one by one they all smiled back. Except for Shirley.

Tess clapped in delight. "We're so happy for you, Ruth! This is wonderful news."

"I'm so nervous though," Ruth confessed, sinking onto a chair beside Phil and resting her arms on the table. "What if he hates me? He thinks I married someone else and didn't wait for him."

"Oh!" Phil gasped as the truth finally hit him. He glared at Shirley. Shirley refused to meet his, or anyone's gaze. She sat still, barely breathing. Phil said, "But that would mean Shirley—"

"Yes, well," Ruth muttered, not wanting to go into details.

He cut her off. "That's a *horrible* thing to do to someone." His tone was soft, but a thread of fury edged each word. "Even more so when it's your *own* sister. How *could* you, Shirley?"

Shirley rocked, an inch forward and back, her cheeks flaming red, her breath catching.

Norma sat back awkwardly, as if realizing she knew the whole story, but didn't speak a word.

"Why didn't you just burn them?" Doreen asked in astonishment. "Why leave them for someone to find you out?"

"Because he was her heart, and I couldn't destroy that," Shirley whispered. Her head snapped around, her gaze meeting Ruth's directly for the first time. "I did the most atrocious thing imaginable, and I don't expect or deserve your forgiveness."

"I should hope not!" Phil sputtered.

Ruth reached out to reassure him. "Phil, it's okay. I finally understand why she did it, and that's between her and I. I'll never forget this, but I hope one day I can forgive it."

Shirley sat there, struggling not to cry. Ellie could only imagine how she must feel having the horrible deed finally revealed, but having it done in front of her friends must be shameful.

After a few deep breaths, Shirley wiped the tears with the handkerchief Phil tossed her way, and nodded her head. "I don't deserve forgiveness, Ruth. I know that." She sat up straight. "I know you don't like to drive. So, I would like to be the one to take you to see Jeremy."

Ruth studied her sister, the shaking hands, the tear-filled eyes, and the paleness that replaced the flushed embarrassment. "Ellie is driving me tomorrow, but you can come if you want."

Shirley nodded.

"But if you do *anything* to ruin this for me, Shirley, I'll never speak to you again." The words were slow and spaced out, as if each one could be a nail in a coffin of their lives together.

"And now," said Ellie as she put her briefcase on the table in front of them, "let's learn a bit about ethics in genealogy."

They all looked at one another, and then at Ruth and Shirley before Ruth said, "Just what we need in our lives, some ethics." She stole a glance at her sister. "And how do we go about that?"

Maggie interrupted them with a tray of cookies that she placed on the table. Pete followed with a large pot of tea, and Maggie returned with cups and sugar and milk. "Now," she said, gazing at each of the seniors slowly, "these cookies are straight from the oven and you have to let them cool. You'll sleep better tonight if you do." She winked at Ellie and headed back to Pete at the counter, gave him a quick kiss before staring after him like a star struck teenager as he left the Café.

The seniors caught the whole encounter, nudged one another, and grinned.

"So." Ellie glanced around. "Since we're writing our own histories, we'll be mentioning other people throughout. Whether it's your parents, siblings, extended family, friends, or co-workers, other people will pop up. And once you've decided whether you'll share your story with others or keep it private, consider how you should portray other people in your life."

"You mean not show how mean someone was to you?" asked Phil. Ellie could see he was fighting the urge to look at Shirley.

Like Phil, Ellie resisted looking at her but heard her shift in her seat. "Exactly. I'm sure we've all been hard done by at some point in our lives, but that doesn't mean you paint the person who delivered the blow as totally black. Be honest, tell the story exactly as it happened. There'll be times when you might exaggerate about your lives, we all do, but what do you gain by depicting someone from your past as a villain?"

"Sometimes it's good," said Lennie. "To get it out, you know."

Ruth sat quietly, her fingers drumming on the table. "Or you could write it out in all its gory details, cuss them out and make it as nasty as you want, then destroy that piece of paper. Try it again when you're calmer and are better able to share the event properly."

"That's a great idea, Ruth!" Ellie nodded at her, and finally stole a glance at Shirley.

Without hesitation, Shirley took a pen and paper and pushed it towards her sister. "I'd be grateful if you could do that. I don't know if it would help us, but it might help you."

They all froze.

Ruth leaned forward and poured herself a cup of tea. "Shirley," she started, aware that everyone was hanging on to her every word, "I've already done that. More than once, in fact. I've lost sleep over it, and my heart has crumpled. It'll take time to process everything. As long as you realize life will never be the same between us, we might have a chance."

"I need a cookie!" Phil declared, grabbing one and eating it in one a bite.

***

When they'd finished their snacks, Ellie held up a hand to get everyone's attention. "I have one other thing I wanted to leave you with tonight."

"Homework?" grumbled Lennie, flicking cookie crumbs off his fingers.

"Exactly." Ellie took a piece of paper from her briefcase and laid it out in the middle of the table. "This is the floor plan for the first house I ever lived in." They all leaned forward to catch a glimpse.

"Seems big," Doreen said, tilting her head to read the writing that indicated each room.

"Well, my parents thought there'd be more children than just me when they bought it," Ellie said. "The key is when I was drawing up this plan, I remembered we had a pantry off the kitchen where my mother let me build forts. Had I not drawn this plan, I doubt I'd have remembered that."

"Is this to jog our memories?" Phil asked.

"It is." Ellie was happy that Phil was engaging more with the group. "Don't worry about it being perfect, or even if you get it all right."

"Do you want us to do all the homes we've lived in?" Tess asked.

"That would be ideal, because you experienced unique life events in each home. Begin with a rough draft, put in what you remember, then let it percolate in your mind for a bit."

"I'll never remember what the house looked like," Phil said.

"I took out some old photos of when I was young," said Ellie. "I found a lot of them taken in that house, and I was able to calculate where the rooms were situated."

"That's a lot of work!" Doreen said.

"You can draw them all at once, or focus on one at a time. It's your choice," said Ellie.

"I think I'll like this homework." Lennie gave one of his rare smiles.

"Oh, my." Doreen pointed to him. "You've got a gold tooth, how fancy!"

Lennie pulled his lips tight together, but failed at his attempt to look grumpy. He ended up laughing along with the others.

"I always knew you were highfalutin," Phil mumbled, still giving Shirley the side-eye and shaking his head.

Ellie tried to pull them all back to the topic. "So, are we agreed? Can we see at least one rough floor plan from everyone next time? And maybe a memory it conjured up?"

"Even the bad ones," Ruth said, staring at her sister.

Chapter Twenty-Four

The smell of bacon in the morning was one of Ellie's guilty pleasures. Each Saturday, she used to make blueberry pancakes with bacon on the side, and a huge bowl of strawberries for Adam and Winnie for breakfast. It was a family ritual that started their weekends off perfectly.

She missed that. She missed them.

Her step faltered as she neared the kitchen, fully expecting to see Quinn with an apron around his waist, spatula in hand at the stove.

"Hey," came a deep voice from behind her. "That smells amazing!"

She whirled to see Quinn walking in the front door, Cali at his heels. So that must mean...

"I hear you two," Ruth called from the kitchen. "Come set the table, please."

Ellie and Quinn found Ruth scooping out eggs and bacon onto a platter, then putting toast onto the cutting board. "Quinn, would you butter these, please?" She nudged the slices towards him and nodded at the butter on the counter.

Ellie grabbed the utensils and took the orange juice from the fridge, all the while sneaking quick glances at Ruth. Ellie caught Quinn's eye when he brought the toast to the table. They exchanged questioning looks and grins. Seeing Ruth so full of energy and life was good for the soul.

"I let Cali out earlier," Ruth said, waving at the large platter. Quinn grabbed it and put it near the toast. "I guessed she'd make it over to the barn to see if you were awake."

Ellie filled Cali's bowl with the dog's breakfast and they all took their seats.

Ruth took a piece of toast. "I can't believe how nervous I feel." Her words were quiet, but they ran together in a jumble. "I'm not even sure I should do this. But if I don't, I'll never know, right?"

Ellie said, "It'll be fine. His son sounds nice, and he said his dad was very excited to see you again."

Ruth chewed her toast listlessly. It was as if all her energy had vanished while making breakfast. "What a mess this has become."

"I don't agree," Quinn said. "I think you're the luckiest person I know, getting a second chance." Ruth opened her mouth to speak, but he shook his head to stop whatever she was about to say. "Sure, it's late in life, but some people never get that first love, ever. Sometimes it takes a long time to find them." He side glanced at Ellie and caught her staring at him. "You're allowed to be scared, nervous, curious, excited, anything and everything. This is big, Ruth, and I wish I could go with you, make sure he's worthy of you."

She shifted her shoulders and gathered herself as he spoke, catching his peek at Ellie. "You're right. Here I am moping about what could have been. What happened, happened. I can't change it. But I can deal with the now."

Ellie grinned. "You've been reading Eckhart Tolle." Ellie knew the book well. Ruth had given her *The Power of Now* after the death of her family. Sometimes she'd read one page a night, sometimes nothing for a week or more, then finally she had devoured it. It had helped ground her in the present, though the pain remained. Only time would ease the pain.

"I do love that book!" Ruth said. "I shall be in the now, and I refuse from this moment to worry about the future. It'll do whatever it wants, with my blessing or without. And how is your work going?" She surprised Quinn with a quick change of topic.

"Almost done. I fixed the flaw." The two women stared at him; eyebrows raised. "Okay, I fixed my mistake, and even though the client is good with the delay, I want it in on time, like I promised."

"Promises are important," Ruth pronounced. "To yourself and to others."

"My, but we're getting so philosophical this morning," Ellie joked.

"What promise have you made to yourself?" Ruth held her gaze, daring her to answer what her heart was really feeling.

"I promised myself to look after those I love," Ellie answered quickly. Too quickly. Ruth raised an eyebrow at her, and Ellie lowered her eyes. "And I promised to let certain people get closer to me."

"Certain people?" Quinn prompted.

"His name is Quinn," Ruth declared as she rose and pushed in her chair, ignoring Ellie's shock. "We'll do the dishes when we get back, I'd probably drop them if I tried now." She headed out of the room and called back over her shoulder. "I won't be long."

"Certain people?" Quinn asked again, leaning back in his chair until it was balancing on two legs.

Ellie fussed with her napkin and crumpled it. She took courage from the kindness in his expression and assured herself that she could do this. The words needed to be said—especially to him—and right now. "It's taken me a long time to trust that I won't die of a broken heart. I nearly did, or it sure felt like it. Losing loved ones is not something you ever forget, but I think I'm ready for more."

"You sound surprised." Quinn moved forward—and closer.

"I *am* surprised." She chuckled, also moving towards him—the jug of juice between them. "I'm pretty sure I wouldn't have moved on just yet without meeting you as we did, at least not right now. I'm ready to—"

With a low woof, Cali scrambled for the door. Ellie followed. She found Shirley sitting rock-still on the porch swing, wearing sensible clothes, her purse clutched in both hands. Ellie held the door open. "Shirley, come in. Would you like some breakfast?"

"No, thank you, Ellie," Shirley said quietly, "I've eaten and I'll wait here if you don't mind." Ellie noticed the dark circles under her eyes and the droop of her mouth, a sign of a restless night.

"I'm ready!" Ruth walked into the room and noticed Shirley through the window.

"You smell nice," Quinn said. "And you look lovely."

"It's Chantilly," Ruth beamed. "Jeremy bought it for me for our last Christmas together. Well, not this bottle, but you know." She blushed and pulled her sweater around her, straightening her skirt and fixing her seams. She had taken the time to dress up a bit for this momentous meeting. "Are you ready?" she asked Ellie, obviously eager to get this day started.

"Yup." Ellie grabbed her purse and keys from the hall table, and gave Quinn a quick kiss. "See you later."

"Ruth." Quinn gave her a big hug. "Enjoy this day. I can't wait to hear all about Jeremy."

She hugged him back, then grabbed Ellie by the arm, steering her out of the house. "Come on, Shirl," Ruth called to her sister as she and Ellie reached the car. "I'm riding shotgun."

***

The drive to the seniors home took less than thirty minutes, but it felt like hours to Ellie. Shirley sat like a statue in the backseat, not speaking, hardly moving, while Ruth chatted non-stop about the weather.

Ellie let her. If that's what she needed, then so be it.

When they drove along the long, winding driveway to the parking lot, Ruth became quiet. She gazed out the window at the landscaped lawns, overflowing flower pots, abundance of benches and the forest beyond. She smiled.

"Oh, my, what a nice place," she said with a sigh.

"I'm not moving into a home!" Shirley exclaimed.

"Neither am I," Ruth answered. "But I'm glad Jeremy has such a wonderful place to live."

"I bet it's a dump inside," Shirley mumbled.

Ellie parked and whirled around to face Shirley. "That's quite enough! You're here because Ruth is a kind soul. I think she should have come alone."

The colour rose in Shirley's cheeks, but she remained miraculously quiet.

Ruth took her time getting out of the car. She watched an elderly woman being pushed by a young attendant, both of them deep in an animated conversation. "Come on Shirley, let's see what kind of dump this is."

"I'll stay here," Shirley mumbled. She turned away from the resident and her attendant, now both laughing at a shared joke. She seemed determined to find fault.

"That's for the best," Ellie agreed, making sure all the windows were wide open before joining Ruth on the path to the front door. Ellie took a quick glance back to see Shirley take a tissue out of her sleeve and wipe her eyes.

The reception area was bright and full of plants, comfy chairs, and a bulletin board covered in notices for activities. A large desk filled the right-side area, and a young lady glanced up from her papers to greet them with a warm smile. "Hello there, how can I help you?"

Before they could answer, a middle-aged man came dashing down the hall and halted in front of them, puffing slightly. He stared at Ruth and grinned from ear to ear. "Ruth, you must be Ruth!" He took her hand in his and gently shook it, before smiling at Ellie. "Hi, I'm Sam."

Ellie shook his hand and immediately knew whatever happened next would work out. This man exuded happiness from the depth of his smile, to the warmth and strength of his grip, to the enthusiasm surrounding him. "I can't believe how excited Dad is. He's actually much better than yesterday, and his energy shocked the staff. Give me a minute to let him know you're here, and I'll be right back." He took off at an easy jog and disappeared into a room near the end of the hall.

Ruth grabbed Ellie's arm in a death grip and leaned in. "Oh, Ellie, maybe this is a mistake. Maybe he—"

Ellie whispered in her ear. "Did you see how excited Sam was? Imagine how Jeremy is feeling! He's probably just as nervous, maybe more so. You can do this Ruth, and I'll be right here."

"Oh, no," Ruth said. "Go outside and get Shirley out of that car. Take her for a walk or something, but don't let her sit there." When Ellie looked like she would argue, Ruth shook her head. "It's not an option, my dear. I'll be going home soon, and I don't want to have to take care of my sister because she's taken ill. She needs fresh air, and to know she's not alone."

"You're very forgiving."

"I haven't forgiven anything," Ruth said. "That might take a long time, if ever. But Quinn is right. She's my sister, the only family I have left in the world, and we'll get through this, somehow." Out of the corner of her eye, she saw Sam beckoning her. She patted her hair and fussed with her skirt, took deep breath and a single step forward.

"You look lovely, Ruth," Ellie assured her, urging her to go.

"I don't know how long I'll be." Ruth hesitated. "Please—come to the door at least." She reached out a hand and Ellie took it. Ruth's hand trembled and when they reached the door, she stopped dead.

Jeremy sat on a couch by the window, dressed smartly in a blue shirt and cardigan, pressed pants and shiny shoes. He raised his head and took a deep sniff, seeing her in the doorway. "Ruthie! I'd know that perfume anywhere!"

Ruth walked in slowly, and tentatively sank onto the edge of the chair Sam had placed facing Jeremy. Jeremy stretched out and took her hands in his, a catch in his voice. "Oh, Ruthie, I've missed you so much!"

Chapter Twenty-Five

Ellie and Sam left Jeremy and Ruth alone and walked back towards the front door.

"Did I mention how happy I am that you found us? Like I told you, my mom died when I was young, and honestly, I don't remember her, but Dad kept her alive with pictures and stories. As much as I knew he loved her, his stories changed as I was growing up, and he would accidentally let something out about Ruth and his life before Mom."

"Did that bother you?"

"No." He shrugged his shoulders. "Mom was like a ghost to me my whole life, but Ruth, well, Ruth seemed real. At times I dreamt Ruth was my mom, and we'd find her one day and everything would be all right." He paused. "Not that things weren't fine. Dad was an amazing father. We were a team."

"He never remarried?" Ellie felt an ache in her chest to think of the man Ruth had loved being alone all those years. Just as Ruth had been.

"I asked him about that once." They arrived at the reception desk and stepped aside to let the older woman in the wheelchair and her attendant go by. The woman wiggled her fingers at them and said good day as she passed. "He finally told me on my wedding day that there had been one true love in his life, and that was Ruth. He was content with his lot, had hobbies, friends, but his heart belonged to Ruth."

"That's so romantic," she said as they walked outside.

"No." He shook his head with force. "What's happening in that room right this minute is romantic!" He checked his phone. "I'm really sorry, but I have to run." He held out his hand. "Do you think Ruth will visit again?"

"I doubt you could keep her away," Ellie answered with a laugh, and shook his hand good bye before he dashed off to his car. If Jeremy was anything like his son, then Ruth was a lucky lady indeed. And perhaps some of that luck had rubbed off on herself and Quinn. She grinned at the thought of moving forward with the handsome woodworker staying in her barn.

A slamming car door startled her. She saw Shirley put a steadying hand on the roof of her car and look around uncertainly. Ellie ran to her. "Shirley, are you okay?"

Shirley nodded. "I needed to stretch my legs a bit. I'm not used to sitting so long in one place."

Ellie grabbed a bottle of water from the front seat. "Here you go." She passed it to Shirley, who drank deeply before handing it back.

"Come on." Ellie held out her hand. After a slight hesitation, Shirley allowed Ellie to take her arm, and they strolled slowly around the grounds.

"We have to stay in the front," Shirley said, glancing often at the main entrance as if Ruth would appear any minute.

"We will, but I think she'll be there for a little while yet." Ellie guided her around a path for a few minutes and then towards a bench in the shade of an enormous maple tree, in direct view of the front door. "Here's a pleasant spot."

Shirley squirmed a bit on the hard bench. "I hope it's not too long because this seat will put my derriere to sleep in a few minutes."

Ellie wasn't sure if Shirley was making a joke or not, but laughed out loud anyway. When the older woman grinned, Ellie realized with sadness how very little she knew about Shirley. Ruth was integral to Ellie in all aspects of her life, as a teacher, a mentor, a saviour when her family had died. But Shirley was, well, Shirley—in the background, bossing Ruth around, pushy, cool and aloof.

But maybe that wasn't Shirley at all. Everyone had a shadow, and maybe what she had shown people all these years wasn't the real Shirley at all, but merely her shadow.

***

"Can I get you something to drink, water, juice?" Jeremy asked, his hands fluttering around as if needing to latch onto something.

"No, I'm fine," she said quietly.

"You look so beautiful, Ruthie." He beamed at her.

"Well, I didn't have these wrinkles last time you saw me, so you must be blowing smoke as the youngsters say, but thank you!"

"Your eyes are still the same deep blue. I've yet to see that shade in anyone else, and when I see it out in the wild, I think of you."

She was nearly in tears seeing how happy he was to see her. He didn't understand her upset and clasped her hands tight. "Ruthie, dear, don't cry! This is such a wonderful day to see you again."

"I didn't marry anyone, Jeremy," she blurted out.

He jerked in surprise. "What? But Shirley told me..."

"Shirley lied—about everything." She pulled out a tissue and wiped her eyes. "I never got your letters, not a one. Shirley hid them, after she *read* them."

Jeremy frowned, his head shaking from side to side. "You didn't know I had come back... to ask you to marry me?"

"No."

He took her hands in his and pulled her up, his step faltering as he guided her to sit close to him on the seat by the window.

"What's wrong, are you injured?"

"No," he assured her, keeping her hand tightly in his as they sat down, their hips touching. "Sam wants me to have an operation. It's my knee. The doctor says my quality of life would improve greatly." He said the last bit with air quotes. "I'm in great health, but I don't want to go under the knife. Sam would need to be there during recovery, and he's got his own family, and then I'd need physiotherapy and—"

"Being able to walk around without pain would be wonderful for you," Ruth said. "I walk every day, rain or shine. I live in the Tiny House Haven community in Percyville, and it's a lovely place to walk."

"I've heard about it, driven past often, but never stopped." Jeremy said. "You've been this close all these years? Shirley said you moved away, and I didn't want to bother you in your new life by searching for you."

"No new life, just the same old one."

He bowed his head. "I never forgot you, even when I married. I felt horrible still loving you and agreeing to marry Louise. When she died, I was sure it was because of something I had done, or not done, not given my all to her."

"Jeremy." She pressed her forehead to his. "I believe things happen for a reason. We both got something precious. You had a loving wife and a wonderful son, and I became a teacher and met so many amazing children, watched them grow, and became part of their lives."

"You never married or had children of your own?" He pulled back, studying her. "Was there not a single man who appealed to you?"

"Only one." She smiled at him.

He put his arm around her shoulder and pulled her closer. They sat quietly, enjoying the warmth of each other. "Do you know why Shirley did it?" he asked.

"There was a big misunderstanding," Ruth said, not wanting to voice the details right then.

"I think she was jealous," Jeremy said. "Did you know she made a pass at me once?"

"When was that? What happened?"

Jeremy quirked a smile at her and winked. "Do you remember that last time in the treehouse?"

She knew exactly what he was talking about, days before he left, their one and only time together. When she became pregnant. Should she tell him about the miscarriage, about the fear and pain she endured all those years ago? A sorrow shared is a sorrow halved.

"I do remember that night," she said. "I have something to tell you, and I don't want you to get upset. I've dealt with it and it's done, but I want you to know."

"This sounds serious." He angled his body as best he could to see her face.

"I got pregnant that night."

Jeremy's eyes flew open wide, and his breath caught. "We have a...."

"No, no!" She cupped his cheeks gently and shook her head. "No, I'm so sorry, I lost the baby a few months on."

Jeremy gazed at the woman before him. "You are such a strong woman, Ruthie. You waited, alone, never knowing what had happened to me, and you faced life with no one by your side, and now you're concerned for me! You are amazing, and I'm so sorry I believed Shirley's lies."

"She can be convincing."

They sat back in the seat, arms locked, fingers entwined, heads touching. What might have been didn't matter at this point. They were together now, where they had always wanted to be, side by side.

A short while later a woman walked into the room carrying a tray of food. "Lunch time, Mr. Butler." She paused when she saw he had company. "Should I make up another tray?"

Ruth checked her watch and shook her head. "No, thank you. My friends are waiting for me outside. And I think you've had enough excitement for one morning." The woman placed the tray beside Jeremy and left.

Jeremy stood, then swayed slightly on his bad leg, letting Ruth take his arm to steady him. "I think I *will* have that knee operation," he announced. "I would very much like to visit you and walk some time."

"That would be wonderful." She stepped into his arms and they let the years drop away, their hearts beating off kilter with age and excitement. They shared a kiss, light, sweet, a new beginning kind of kiss. Ruth took a step back first.

"Will you visit again?" Jeremy asked, slipping back into the seat and rubbing his knee.

"Every day if you'll let me."

"Then every day it shall be." He grinned at her, his eyes sparkling. "I'll get that surgery scheduled lickity-split. The doctor said he could fit me in, because of my age."

"I guess there's something to be said for advanced years." Ruth leaned in to hug him again. "I can't believe I've found you, Jeremy. I don't want to leave at all right now!"

He looked over at his bed. "I don't think we'd both fit in that though."

She laughed and swatted his arm. "Still the same, I see."

"With you, always."

"I'll be back tomorrow then. Can I bring you anything?" She didn't want to step outside and leave the cocoon of this room. What if the bubble burst? What if... what if amazing things happened in the days to come? Yes, that was exactly what she would think of.

"Just you, and maybe a croissant from the Cozy Corner. I'm not supposed to, but I do so love Maggie's baking."

"You know Maggie?" She was astonished.

"Who doesn't?" He finally made the connection and grinned. "Small world, isn't it?"

"Tomorrow then." She waved and walked out of the room.

"Counting the minutes," he called after her.

Chapter Twenty-Six

"She's going to leave me," Shirley whispered. "She's going to move in here to be with him."

Ellie took her hand, surprised that Shirley squeezed it tight instead of snatching it away. "I don't think Ruth would like to live her life on a schedule, do you? And most retirement homes have rules."

They were quiet for a minute. "She doesn't enjoy being told what to do," Shirley nodded, as if this was the key to the future. "Do you know, I asked her once to fold the towels a certain way, and she refused!" Shirley turned to Ellie as if expecting her to agree Ruth was at fault.

"Well." Ellie searched for the right response. "If you don't like how she does it, you could do it yourself, then you wouldn't get mad at her."

Shirley sat in silence, barely aware of the birds hopping about the ground around their bench, beaks diving into the grass searching for delicacies. "That's a good idea," she mumbled.

"No one likes being told what to do, I guess." Ellie sat back, her shoulder grazing Shirley's, gazing up into the tree above her, shading her eyes with her palm against the sun streaming through the leaves.

"Do you enjoy living alone?" Shirley asked.

Ellie had to think about that. "I'm the queen of my castle," she replied, brushing a stray leaf from her jeans. "But you know what, Shirley? I do get lonely. Cali's a lovely companion but..."

"Quinn seems nice." Shirley was grinning now—another surprise. "He's rather... appealing, and his Scottish accent can make your knees wobble."

A blush crept up Ellie's cheeks, but she was saved from further comments when Shirley blurted "There she is!". She jumped up, and sped toward the front door, Quinn and all his attributes instantly forgotten. "Come on!"

Ruth was walking out the front door, a spring in her step, shoulders straight, and her head held high. She looked ten years younger.

***

"Sorry I'm late," Quinn called as he ran into the house, the front door slamming behind him. "That smells so good!" He stopped at the kitchen entrance in surprise.

Calmly, Ellie handed him a large bowl of shrimp pasta. After a moment of hesitation, he placed it in the middle of the table. There were four place settings and the fourth person at the table was Shirley.

"We've been waiting for you," admonished Shirley lightly. "Ruth has refused to tell the story more than once, and she insisted you should be here."

Ellie and Quinn exchanged hooded glances before taking their seats across from the sisters. Quinn said, "I just dropped off the last pieces to the client, *on time.*" He nodded to Ruth and smiled. "I stayed to organize it all for them. It took a little longer than I thought it would."

"I'm sure they were delighted," Ruth replied, spooning out a generous portion of pasta, avoiding everyone's eager gazes.

"So, Ruth spent some time with Jeremy today," Ellie finally prompted.

"Some time?" Shirley mumbled. "More like half an hour!"

"Hardly enough time after all these years." Ruth stared at her sister, waiting for more comments, but none came.

Quinn's gaze darted from the sisters to Ellie. He raised his eyebrows in question. Ellie gave a miniscule shrug and helped herself to a piece of garlic bread.

"Okay." Ruth sat forward. "You've all been so patient. First, I won't be seeing Jeremy—"

"Are you kidding me?" Shirley dropped her fork with a noisy clatter. "After *all this time*, now he doesn't want to—"

Ruth slapped her hand on the table to end Shirley's rant. "Stop that! I'm saying I won't be seeing him every day because he's having surgery. Knee problem—that's why he was in the chair. He's been resisting the surgery, but now he wants to go through the whole therapy process and be able to walk properly. *For me.*" She smiled at them all, as if this was the most wonderful present she had ever received.

"Wow." Quinn froze with his pasta halfway to his mouth. "You mean he wouldn't have gone for it at all?"

"No." Ruth covered her mouth as she finished her last bite, excited to continue her story. "I told him I wanted to walk with him. I'm a big walker, and I want him beside me."

"When do you walk?" Shirley asked in surprise.

"Whenever you go for groceries, do your gardening for people, take a nap, or a long bath. I either walk around the lake, or I come over to visit Ellie."

"You cross the highway?" Shirley practically sputtered her astonishment.

"Never at peak traffic times, and I can scoot across rather quickly." Ruth appeared very proud of that ability.

"Why didn't you ever ask me to come with you?"

"Because you don't like to walk for long periods and..." Ruth hesitated, searching for the right words, "And sometimes I need time to myself."

Shirley shifted her attention to her plate, moved the strands of pasta around, considering her sister's comment. "I guess I *can* be a bit much."

"And sometimes I just need time to myself," Ruth repeated.

"Okay," Quinn said. "I can't take much more of this. What's the story? Where has he been, what's going on?"

Ruth looked at each of them solemnly. "He loves me."

"Who wouldn't!" Ellie shook her head as if this was the most obvious thing in the world.

"No," Ruth said softly, "that's wrong. He never *stopped* loving me. For all these years."

"Did he tell you what I..." Shirley stopped, hanging her head with shame. "Did he tell you what I told him?"

"He did." Ruth cocked her head, as if hearing again what Jeremy had told her. "Your words crushed him. He left town that day and moved out west where he met his wife. When she died a couple of years after Sam was born, he moved back to Montreal. And since you had told him I had moved away, he didn't try to find me. He thought I was a married woman with a family of my own. But he picked the retirement home up here because it was the closest he could get to where we had met. But he never imagined I'd still be here."

Shirley gently placed her fork on her plate, her hand shaking, and closed her eyes. "You cannot believe how sorry I am, Ruth." Her voice shook, and wayward tears flowed down her face, falling to her plate.

Ruth passed her a napkin, unable to respond in a civil manner.

"He must hate me so much," Shirley whispered, dabbing at her tears.

"He is incapable of hating anyone." Ruth toyed with a piece of bread. "We did agree on one thing though. We have no clue what our lives would have been like together, no doubt amazing, but we would not have had the lives we do have." She took a bite, chewing slowly, lost in thought. "I wouldn't have become a teacher... or met all the amazing children I taught. I wouldn't have met Ellie... And Jeremy wouldn't have his son, whom he loves more than life itself."

"But..." Shirley said.

"No buts." Ruth held up her hand, the teacher in her never far away. "We can only move on. Things have to change, Shirley."

Shirley pushed her plate away. "In what way?"

"I'm staying here tonight, and I'll be home tomorrow after Ellie and I go to school. I expect the house to be in good shape."

Shirley's eyes squinted and her nose scrunched as if she suddenly smelled something she didn't like.

"I know you don't enjoy housework, but news flash, Shirley—*nobody* likes housework, but we all know it has to be done. It's time you helped me out. And you need to learn to cook."

"Well..." Shirley wasn't agreeing just yet.

"And I'll be seeing Jeremy often, so I'll need a lift. And when he's able, I want him to come and visit us at home."

Shirley sat still, locking and unlocking her fingers, listening to her sister's comments before putting her napkin on the table and standing up. "Now that you've sorted our lives out, I best head home and get started."

"I won't be there till lunch. No need to tire yourself out. Get a good sleep. I want you healthy." Ruth hugged her sister tight, ninety-two years of love not easy to erase. "I'm sure it'll work out," she whispered into Shirley's ear. "I'm going to need time."

Quinn wolfed down the rest of his meal quickly and stood. "Come on Shirley, I'll drive you home." He winked at Ellie. She knew he'd take care of Shirley.

Shirley stopped at the door, as if an afterthought. "Thank you for the meal, Ellie. It was delicious."

Pleasantly surprised, Ellie replied, "Any time, Shirley."

Ruth and Ellie waited while Quinn and Shirley drove off, then they both let their shoulders slump, as if a possible storm had been avoided.

Cali nudged Ruth, and she stepped outside with the dog. "I'm taking Cali for a walk."

Ellie watched the pair until they disappeared into the forest, then strolled back to a kitchen full of dishes, pushed-out and abandoned chairs, and half-eaten meals.

A seed of unease rested in her core. Was it just because of tomorrow's ordeal at the school, or was it the final look in Shirley's eyes as she walked out the door?

Chapter Twenty-Seven

Quinn was making breakfast when Ellie entered the kitchen. She could get used to someone cooking her meals, especially Quinn. It felt comfortable having him move from fridge to stove, cracking eggs and dropping bread in the toaster, moving like a well-coordinated machine.

"If you're just gawking at my superb physique, make yourself useful and set the table," he said.

"Feeling full of yourself, I see." Ellie was thankful he couldn't see how red she had gone, because that's exactly what she had been doing. She made noise getting the utensils out and finished by putting the juice on the table. As she reached for the jam in the fridge, Quinn stepped in front of her and drew her in for a good morning kiss.

"Now this is how you should begin a morning," he growled into her ear, then nibbled her neck. She melted into him, forgetting she was standing in her own kitchen with Ruth sleeping down the hall.

"Children!" So, Ruth wasn't sleeping after all. "I think there's a time and place for that and since I'm hungry, this is neither that time nor place."

Ellie disentangled from Quinn's arms, though he kept his arm around her shoulder, their hips touching. "Well, I..."

"My fault." Quinn smirked at Ruth, as if he would do it all again should she step out of the room. "There'll be more of that later, so buckle up."

Ruth smacked him soundly on the arm. "Thank goodness I'm leaving soon." But the hug she gave Ellie contradicted her words. "Thank you so much for everything you've done."

"After what you did for me? There's no comparison. We're here for each other." Ellie moved to her chair and passed Ruth the platter of toast. "And I can't wait to meet Jeremy!"

"Me too." Quinn placed the bacon and eggs on the table and took his seat. "If he can make you this happy, I think I'll give him an unconditional thumbs up."

"And you." Ruth's tone was serious when she pinned Quinn with a look. "What are you planning to do now you've finished your project?"

"That depends on this one." He motioned to Ellie.

"This one?" Ellie squeaked. "*This one* has a name, you know."

"What would you like to do?" Ruth wouldn't drop the subject.

Quinn took the bait. "I would like to make more sizeable pieces of furniture because there's a market for them, and I love doing them." He finished his eggs and speared a piece of bacon with his fork. "And I would like to continue renting the barn for as long as I can. And I would like to spend time here, and in Montreal. And I would like to court Ellie, if she would like that."

"Court?" Ellie grinned like a teenager on a first date. "Oh, I think courting might be fun." She eyed him mischievously.

"But you'll stay in the barn while you're here, correct?" Ruth clarified.

Ellie and Quinn nodded quickly.

"Of course, I will, Ruth," Quinn agreed. "Whatever Ellie and I have right now, we'll move at her pace and..."

"Oh, for goodness sake," Ruth said, laughing at their discomfort. "I was kidding. Life is too short to wait when you know something's right. Don't make that mistake. Grab life by the buttocks and squeeze!"

"Ruth!" Ellie gasped.

Quinn leaned back in his seat and nodded, his gaze never leaving Ellie. "You're absolutely right."

"Time to go," Ruth called as she headed to the door and picked up her purse.

***

Silence greeted Ellie as she walked into the classroom. All heads swiveled her way; all eyes focused on her as she looked around at the abnormally quiet room of students.

"I've got a surprise for you," Mrs. O'Brien informed her class. "I told you Winnie's mom was coming to teach us how to interview people and learn about their lives. Today is the day."

The students stole quick glances at each other, a few squirmed in their seats, but most seemed curious.

Ellie felt glued to the spot inside the door. Ruth pushed past her and gave the teacher a wave before finding a seat at the back of the room. All eyes followed her and whispers floated from child to child.

"And Miss Cotter, who many of you know used to teach in this school—" began the teacher.

"In this very class," Ruth finished for her from the back of the room. "It still has the same icky shade of paint on the walls, I see."

Most of the students laughed, while others were wide-eyed, not sure what to make of this elderly woman invading their space.

Ellie finally stepped up to the desk, as the students relaxed and shifted back to face her. She took a batch of papers from her briefcase and handed them to the first person in each row. "If you could pass these back so everyone gets one, that would be great."

She waited until each student had a paper on their desk. Some of them read the questions, while others just stared at her.

"So..." she started, then stopped. She caught Ruth's nod of encouragement from the back of the room, and her miming action of taking a deep breath. She felt her chest expand as she did the same. "So," she began again, "Mrs. O'Brien asked me to come and talk about interviewing people. As part of your social studies, she thought it would be interesting for you to get to know your parents."

A few quiet groans, and shuffling of feet and fidgeting abounded.

"Oh," she raised a hand to quiet them. "I don't mean your parents as they are now. I mean BC, meaning 'Before Children'. Before you were even a thought in their minds, maybe even before they met each other."

She could tell she had the attention of the girls, but the boys were not engaged.

"Do you know whether your dad ever skipped classes at school?" The boys showed their first interest. Some picked up their pens, and others shook their heads. "What? You don't think your parents did the same things you do?"

A single hand raised in the air. It was Winnie's best friend, Brenda. Ellie's chest tightened, and she blinked back the tears. She grabbed the tissue from her sleeve and crunched it tight. This she'd learned from the best. "Yes, Brenda?"

"Are you okay?" Brenda asked hesitantly.

If it was possible for the air to be sucked out of a classroom, this moment would be it. Everyone sat frozen, breaths held, shocked at Brenda's question. And they all waited for the answer.

Ellie smiled, the tightness in her chest easing as she realized each of these youngsters had lost someone as well, a friend. "Yes," she said. "I'm doing okay. But I want to tell you something. I've known you for years, you've been to our farm, you've eaten meals with our family and the thought of coming here this morning to see you all, terrified me. I'm so sorry. I should have come sooner and let you know it's okay. You know that saying, life goes on? It actually does, slowly. And thank you all for the lovely card you sent."

"You did thank us," Brenda said.

"Not in person, like this, looking at your faces." She took a deep shaky breath. "It meant a lot."

"So how do we get our parents to tell us the truth?" This from a boy at the back of the class.

"That's what we're going to learn about right now." Ellie smiled at them, knowing the tension had vanished and everyone in the room would be okay. Ruth made a "go on" motion with her hands, waiting for her to continue.

"I've written a few basic warm-up questions on the sheets I've handed out." Various heads bent down to read the paper before them. "But..." She waited for all eyes to be back on her. "You can add your own questions about what you want to know."

"What if they say it's none of our business?" asked another girl sitting in front of her, worry lines spreading out across her forehead.

"Respect their privacy if they don't want to answer. But if you let them know it matters to you, they might change their minds. If they don't change their minds, let it be. As you can see from the other questions, they're pretty mild, like where did you go to school, what did you like or hate about school, stuff like that. It's interesting to find out if your parents share any of your likes or dislikes. How about what did they want to be when they were your age? Dreams change, for many reasons."

The class thought about that and Brenda said, "My mom is great at making clothes. She told me last year she had wanted to go to school to become a clothing designer."

"Why didn't she?" asked Ellie.

Brenda focused on the page in front of her, as if ashamed of the answer. "Because she got pregnant with me. But she told me she's thinking of going to night school for it."

"Imagine each of you having homework at the same time!" Mrs. O'Brien said. Brenda smiled at that.

"There are many stories in your parents' lives, and those of you who have grandparents still living, you can talk to them, too. There were no cell phones or internet back in their day. That alone made life different. I remember my parents having a phone attached to the wall, one phone, and you had to dial the number you were calling."

"What?" Said an astonished voice from the side of the room. A young boy was shaking his head, not believing her.

"Here." Ellie took out her phone and punched a few buttons. She walked over to the boy and showed him a picture of an old rotary phone. She pointed to the holes on the dial. "You put your finger in here and turned it all the way to the right, and that's how you dialed." She walked around the classroom, sharing the photo and watching the various disbelieving expressions appear.

"I've always wanted to know what my dad did for fun when he was young," the same boy said from the back of the class. "He says he never did anything, but I don't believe that."

"So maybe that should be the question you ask," Ellie suggested. "Think about this a bit, what specifically do you want to know? You can ask multiple questions, and other questions may come from those answers. Since they know about this project, I'm sure they'll be happy to answer. But always remember to respect another person's privacy. There will be things that people don't want to talk about, because they're embarrassed, or it brings them pain. Don't push."

They filled the rest of the class with a discussion about how life differed from their parents' or grandparents' time to the present. Ruth joined in, regaling them with stories from when she was their age. Then the students grouped together, throwing ideas back and forth about what they wanted to discover.

Ellie glanced back to see Ruth standing by the desk. She looked at the clock on the wall, surprised to see they had gone on longer than the initial hour allotted to the lesson. She gathered her notebook and papers and put them back in the briefcase, and caught the students quieting as they noticed she was leaving.

"Thank you, Mrs. McLellan, for coming and seeing us," Brenda said.

"You're welcome." She smiled at the whole class. "It's been great seeing you all, and I hope you have fun with this project. If you discover any interesting bits of information, I'd love to hear about it."

Ruth took her arm, and they left the room as the children called out their goodbyes.

***

Ruth got out of the car slowly when they parked at the farm. "And now I'll go for a walk to the pond with Cali to stretch my legs." At the sound of her name, Cali left Quinn's side for Ruth's. "I'd like to go home after I get back, if you don't mind. And thank you for fixing the ladder at the treehouse, Quinn."

"Please tell me you won't climb it," he said.

She waved as she left, Cali dashing off ahead of her. Ellie nudged Quinn. "She wouldn't, right?"

He put his arm around her and rested his chin on the top of her head, pulling her closer. "Who knows! That treehouse has some special magic about it." She moved to follow Ruth, but Quinn pulled her back. "No, let her go. She won't do it if she can't. She's got something to live for now."

***

Quinn had a large, wrapped parcel waiting on the front porch when Ruth stepped out of the forest after her walk. He was pacing around it, anxious and excited, and had refused to tell Ellie what it was.

"I mean really," Ellie protested, trying to figure it out from its shape. "It's bigger than a breadbox but..."

"No. It's for Ruth, and I won't say another word."

"And what is this?" Ruth asked, obviously delighted by the prospect of a present.

Quinn motioned to it. "Just a little something I made for you, for old times' sake."

She rested her hand on top of the package, which was as high as her waist, and tore the paper slowly. With each rip a new portion of the gift inside appeared, and by the time it was totally revealed both Ellie and Ruth were grinning like kids at Christmas.

It was Ruth's treehouse, but as a birdhouse.

"Oh, Quinn." Ruth studied the details, her gaze seeking out and finding the initials Jeremy had carved in the ladder days before he had left for the war. "This is too much!"

"I've made a couple for friends, replicas of their homes actually, and the birds love them too." Quinn seemed about ready to burst with pleasure at seeing their reactions. "I thought you might like one as well."

"What an amazing talent you have." Ellie sat on the porch and drank in Quinn's careful workmanship. "Look, Ruth, there's the wobbly last step on the ladder!" She gazed up at Quinn and beamed. "I am *so* impressed."

"I'm glad you like it." Quinn picked it up and headed for the car. "I'll put this anywhere you'd like at your tiny house."

Chapter Twenty-Eight

Ruth had to use her key when they arrived at her house, as the door was locked tight. She turned in surprise to Ellie who was right behind her, Ruth's bag in her hand, while Quinn retrieved the treehouse. "Shirley never locks the door!"

They walked in to find the house sparkling clean. "Shirley?" Ruth called out as she made her way to the kitchen.

Quinn took Ruth's bag from Ellie. "I'll put this in your room." Returning to the kitchen, he said, "Your room is as clean as a whistle, with a vase of fresh flowers on the dresser." He stopped short at seeing Ruth and Ellie. Ruth was reading a note and Ellie's hands were white -knuckled on the back of a chair. "What's wrong?" he asked.

Ruth waved the letter at him. "She's gone! She took the job in Mountainview and left!"

Ellie took the letter and read it aloud. "*I've decided that I don't want to be a third wheel in your new life, and have accepted the job to redo the town's gardens. Don't worry about me, I'll have a place to stay and will send pictures. I hope you have a wonderful life with Jeremy. Your sister, Shirley.*"

"I wasn't planning on leaving her for Jeremy." Ruth sank onto a chair and lowered her head. She sighed, as if she couldn't handle anymore drama right then. She glanced at the cat clock on the wall. "The bus to Mountainview leaves in half an hour from the bus stop. It's the only way she could get there."

"Unless someone offered to drive her," Quinn pointed out.

The two women shot daggers at him. He held his hands up in surrender. "Right," he said pulling out his car keys, "let's head over there right now."

"She can't do this," Ruth muttered as she gathered her purse and followed the others outside. Her hands shook as she fought to lock the door. Ellie took the keys from her and finished the job. "She can't just up and leave."

"Maybe she really believed you were leaving her, Ruth," Ellie said.

"Why in the world would I do that?" Gracelessly, she managed to fit herself into the front seat. "I enjoy my life the way it is." Ellie jumped in the back.

Quinn left the Tiny House Haven and headed for the bus depot, driving a bit too fast, but no one suggested he slow down.

From the backseat, Ellie squeezed Ruth's shoulder. "We'll find her."

The rest of the drive passed in silence, finally shattered by a gasp from Ruth as they pulled in to see Shirley sitting by herself on the hard wooden bench outside the bus depot ticket booth. Her arms were crossed as if to hold herself up, her head drooping from exhaustion. The sleeve of a blouse was sticking out of a hurriedly packed suitcase at her feet.

Quinn squealed to a stop and Ruth pushed on her door to get to her sister. The pair met on the platform, one sitting and dejected, the other slowly easing to sit beside her, hand to her chest as if fighting for breath.

"Ruth, are you okay?" Ellie called out.

Ruth waved her away.

Quinn murmured, "Stop hovering, *Mom*," drawing Ellie with him to a picnic bench under the shade of some trees, the two women still in view.

***

"What are you doing here?" Shirley refused to look at her sister.

"I'm here to take you home," Ruth gasped out. "This is absolutely ridiculous!"

"What is? Me wanting to have a life too?"

"What do you mean too? Nothing has changed." Ruth forced herself to take slower breaths.

"Oh, phooey!" Shirley pretended to focus on a group of young children squealing in delight as they played in a nearby park. "You found a beau, and there's no place in your life for me now."

Ruth leaned back against the wall and stared at the blue sky as if searching for wisdom or guidance. "I'll say it again, Shirley. What you did was the most horrible thing you could ever have done to me. You say you were trying to protect me, but that wasn't your place or your choice."

"But he..." Shirley started, only to be stopped by Ruth's raised hand, now balled into a fist.

"No!" Ruth lowered her arm and struggled for calm. "All my life I've been the one who kept things in check, made sure everyone was okay, and been the mediator in arguments. Not once have my feelings been discussed or considered."

Silence.

"Not once." Ruth reiterated. "I've lost one possible life but I lived another. I refuse to play the game of what ifs with you, Shirley, because I don't know what life would have been like. But I will never forgive the fact that I was not given the choice to decide for myself."

"I understand." Shirley mumbled, wiping the sweat from her forehead.

Ruth wrenched a tissue from her sleeve and shoved it at her sister. "I can't promise I'll ever forgive this. But I do promise I'll be seeing Jeremy, in whatever way we can, for however long we have left."

"I would hope so."

"Would you? What do you really want out of life, Shirley? Do you want to go off and live on your own, doing your gardening? I thought Sara was offering you a landscaping job right on our doorstep at the Tiny House Haven. You're an excellent gardener, and so many people are asking you for help with their designs."

"I didn't think you'd appreciate me being around right now."

Ruth rested her head against the bus depot wall and felt her body tense as the bus pull up in front of them.

Neither moved.

Shirley fidgeted with her ticket, now slightly damp and crumpled in her hand. She made to stand but Ruth pulled her back.

"Don't go, Shirley," Ruth whispered. "Not like this, not now, not ever."

The bus's door swished opened with a groan and the driver raised his shoulders at them in question. Shirley took a long moment then shook her head.

He closed the door, pulling away from the two women on the bench.

***

Quinn and Ellie drove them back to Ruth's, and Quinn carried Shirley's bag into the house.

"I left a little something in the oven for lunch," Shirley said.

"You cooked?" Ruth asked.

"Not much, but enough to get us through." She gave a weak smile, maybe uncertain of her accomplishment.

Ellie wasn't sure what to do, leave them to sort it out or stay and help ease them into things. But she could see the sisters had changed, as if reversing roles. Ruth was stronger, more able to speak her mind and not always needing to spare someone's feelings, especially if that person was hurting her. And Shirley had lost her bluster. There was a calm about her, an acceptance of life and a willingness to adjust to her sister's needs that Ellie thought she'd never see.

"We'll leave you be now." She gave Ruth a quick hug, whispering in her ear, "You can come over any time you want."

Ruth kissed her on the cheek. "I will visit you whenever I please." She moved to Quinn, who slung an arm around her. "And I expect to see amazing things from you." She stepped back and searched his face. "And keep my Ellie safe and happy."

"I'll devote every minute to doing so," he assured her.

"Come on." Ellie grabbed his hand and pulled him toward the door before stopping short and turning back to the sisters. "And Shirley, you're welcome anytime."

As they headed to the car, they heard Ruth say, "Wait till you see what he made for me, Shirley, it's the treehouse! We'll decide where to put it later."

***

The drive back was quiet. Ellie had taken Quinn's hand when they left Ruth's house, and their fingers remained entwined in the car. Cali came running to them when they arrived home, eager for rubs and attention.

"Come with me a second." Quinn pulled her towards the barn. Inside, the light bathed the workspace in brightness. On the main bench was another birdhouse. This one was a miniature of Ellie's farmhouse.

She trailed her fingers across the building, marvelling at the porch swing hanging from slim steel wires, and Cali's bright red ball laying across the wooden boards in front of it. She peered closer and saw a shadow in an upper window, her bedroom to be exact. There was a woman, her hand holding open the curtain slightly as if gazing out.

Ellie shook her head in awe. "This is incredible, Quinn! I can't thank you enough."

"We'll find some place to put it when I get back tomorrow. I have to take care of a few things in town and get more clothes and supplies." He was talking so fast, almost babbling with excitement. "And I need to make sure the house is okay and pick up my mail."

"And you'll sleep in the house when you're here working," Ellie blurted out. "I don't think there's any need to sleep in the barn anymore—you can use Ruth's room."

He tilted her head up towards him. "You're sure about that?"

A smile spread slowly and she nodded. "Yeah, I guess I am." She stood on tiptoe and kissed him. Minutes later they drew apart, breathless, but settled.

"Okay then." He stepped back and looked around the barn. "I'll get my bag and head out now so I can get back quicker." He went one way and then the other, as if not sure what he should do.

Ellie took pity on him and called to Cali. "We'll see you tomorrow then, drive safely." She strode out of the barn with Cali by her side, trying for nonchalance when all she wanted to do was click her heels together and dance.

***

Ellie found Quinn's truck gone after her walk, but the barn full of his tools and materials, the doors wide open. He must have had other things on his mind when he left. She smiled as she locked the big barn doors tight, then with a bounce in her step, she ran up the porch stairs and spent the next twenty minutes doing the dishes and cleaning the kitchen.

Cali followed her down the hall and sat at the door of Ruth's old room while Ellie stripped the bed and remade it for Quinn. She took special care, fluffing the pillows and finding some books from her library he might enjoy, and putting them on the bedside table. She cleaned the bathroom and set out clean towels as well.

"Come on Cali." She grabbed her keys, left the house and locked the door behind her. "Let's go visit Maggie." Together they sprinted through the woods to the highway exit where she pushed the camouflage foliage away and squeezed through. She had adjusted it, leaving it accessible for Ruth to get through for when she wanted to visit, but invisible to any passersby.

The lunch crowd had slowed and the Cozy Corner was quiet mid-afternoon. Ellie took her leash and snapped it onto Cali's collar, leaving plenty of length for the dog to roam around the back of the building. The unfamiliar smells alone would keep her busy for a while.

When she stepped through the front door, she found Maggie sitting at a side table, a document spread out in front of her. Maggie's head popped up when she heard a customer, and when she saw it was Ellie, she dashed over.

"Just the person I wanted to see!" She pulled Ellie to the table, nudging her into the seat a little more forcibly than necessary.

"Well, hello to you too." Ellie grinned at her friend's excitement. "Why yes, I'd love a coffee and cookie, thank you very much." When Maggie didn't respond, Daphne nodded to her and set about getting her order.

"So, this is what I need your expertise with." Maggie pushed the papers across the table. "This is a lawyer's letter telling me my grandmother, who apparently died a month ago, has left me something in her will and would I be able to attend the reading of the will in two days."

"Well, that's awesome!" Ellie shifted back when her coffee and cookie arrived. "Thank you," she said to Daphne who shook her head towards Maggie, showing she'd been in this state for some time.

"That's just it though," Maggie stared, a suspicious glint in her eyes. "My grandmother died before I was born. At least that's what my mom told me. So, who is this?"

THE END

About Author

Beth Farrar has been writing stories since her parents handed her a library card. Her imagination was sparked. Encouragement from English teachers set her on a serious path of learning the craft.

From writing TV scripts to full length movies for pleasure and practice, she developed her writing skills by exploring various mediums. Filling notebooks with ideas, sketching characters and locations, and inventing sticky situations for characters to survive, is Beth's happy place (besides walking in cemeteries, but that's another story).

For fifteen years Beth wrote a monthly column, Living Country, in her local English language newspaper, Main Street, sharing interesting observations of living and raising her three sons in the country with her husband. Having always loved genealogy, Beth melded two of her passions together and created the Ellie McLellan Genealogy Mystery series.

For tips and tricks on how to write your own personal history story, head over to Beth Farrar – Author on Facebook for more information. Or visit her website bethfarrar.com and join her newsletter to get a free Oral History Questions booklet to start your journey writing your own personal story.

Afterword

Would you like to write your own personal story? Head over to my Instagram page at "bethfarrar8115", or my Facebook site at "Beth Farrar – Author". You'll find more tips about how to start putting together your own life story. And join my newsletter at bethfarrar.com.

The seniors in Ellie's genealogy group learned a couple of things during this story that you can apply to your own journey.

1. Searching census returns. Depending on your age, you might be able to find your parents and/or grandparents in various census returns. It would be interesting to know where they were living and what their occupations were.

2. Using Google for various things, such as locating newspaper archives to search. There are many free sites that allow for searches. You might even locate your own birth announcement!

3. Take a road trip back to a location from your youth. If you don't live too far, go for a drive down your old street, take a picture of the home you lived in, and maybe cruise past the school(s) you attended.

4. Making floor plans of homes you lived in. This one is fun. Start with the one you remember the most. See if you have any photos of the house and make a few notes about things you remember most.

Acknowledgments

I've been blessed to have a strong group around me as I wrote this book, and they deserve my deepest thanks.

Ronnie Roberts; my wonderful editor. I appreciate your continued patience, guidance, and taking the time to answer my many questions.

Teresa O'Neil; once again, being an early reader with helpful suggestions. Your recommendations about plot points are truly valuable.

Daphne Petersen; for taking my second book through the crazy winter Christmas storm of 2022 and finding those typos has spared me remarks from readers!

My sons, Liam, Connar and Devlin; you always encouraged me through every step and were delighted to hold the final copy in your hands. Dreams rock!

And my leading cheerleader, my hubby; for believing in me and asking just the right questions at the right time. Your steady support means everything to me.

Family Promises - Book 3

If you enjoyed following Ellie McLellan and her group of senior genealogists solve their mystery, get ready for the next adventure:

We've all jokingly muttered at one point in time, "I wish I had a rich relative somewhere...".

Be careful what you wish for!

When genealogist Ellie McLellan's best friend in the world, Cozy Corner Café bakery owner Maggie Williams, excitedly tells her she's been named as a beneficiary in the will of a relative she's never met, the pair agrees to attend the reading together. Whoo-hoo—Road Trip!

Only, this road opens a door into Maggie's family history she never imagined existed, bringing people into her life that she has every reason to distrust and danger to everyone around her.

Instead of riches, Maggie may have found ruin.

With the Senior Genealogy Group eager to help, Ellie's back in the fray, putting her genealogical skills to the test tracking down the mysteries of Maggie's past before they consume her friend.